DeSai

In The Depths

By
R.W.K. Clark

This is a work of fiction. All names, characters, locales, and incidents are
the product of the author's imagination and any resemblance to actual
people, places or events is coincidental or fictionalized.
Published in the United States by Clarkltd.
Po Box 45313 Rio Rancho, NM 87174
info@clarkltd.com

Edition 1
United States Copyright Office
TX8-281-468 May 2016
Library of Congress Control Number: 2017907100
International Standard Book Numbers
ISBN-10: 0692721932
ISBN-13: 978-0692721933
ASIN: B01GD7CPBA

/200801

CONTENTS

ACKNOWLEDGMENTS

I dedicate this novel to my wonderful readers and for all the amazing people I've met and those I haven't. To my family and loved ones, all your support will not be forgotten.

This book was made possible by reviews from readers like you

Thank you

R.W.K. Clark

PROLOGUE

Since the beginning of time, there have been vampires, and there have been witches. They heard of each other, but they never crossed the path of the other. They never sought to meet, and they never tried to discover what could happen if they joined together the unique powers that they had; they respected the boundaries of the natural order, the order set down since the foundation of the world.

Over time, curiosity got the best of the witches. With each passing generation, the evil and greed for power that filled their hearts made them begin to wonder, did vampires exist? If they did, could they be captured and possessed? Could they be contained by the female species of the order and used to their advantage?

The hearts of women have always been evil; it is for this reason that Satan himself approached Eve first in the Garden of Eden. She could control the man, and it was the man Satan needed to deceive. Without her, there was no hope.

R.W.K. Clark

CHAPTER 1

1796 Honduras

Manuel Jasso sat rigidly, the fire before him, and those fires burning all around him, burning large and bright. It was his watch on this sweltering night, and though the night was still and peaceful, he maintained rapt attention, his head jerking toward even the slightest of sounds. The men around him slept peacefully; how he wished he were one of them or that they did not need to be here at all. Alas, this was not so.

He kept his eyes straining in the darkness as he uncapped his canteen. He brought it to his lips and took a small sip, enjoying just enough of the water inside to wet his tongue and appease his thirst for a moment. He recapped it and let it fall back to its place against his chest, hanging from the worn leather strap around his neck.

It was unusually hot tonight, hotter than he could ever remember in all of his 36 years. It was a heat that sat on the surface of the skin and soaked through the skin. He wondered fleetingly if it were an omen if it meant the one they hunted was nearby. It was always hotter when the beast was in one's midst.

The monster must be captured, must be stopped. Last year, alone, forty women and seventeen men had gone missing from Olanchito, and only last week, they had received word that the recently established village of La Ceiba had begun to have the same nightmare. The council knew what was happening and who was doing the bidding: the man and his victims themselves. There was but one way to stop it, and that was to capture and destroy the man who had started it all.

They only knew him as Comte DeSai. He had settled in a massive abandoned homestead, five years ago, outside Olanchito. Initially, his presence was construed by the townspeople as a blessing. He was active in doing good for the town, and he became a regular face at council meetings and town gatherings. He began a vineyard and ventured to make fine wines, and the wine was very good by all accounts. He had brought some of the very best of his wares with him when he came and shared it willingly. Perhaps, Olanchito would prosper, after all.

But then the head councilman's wife had gone missing. DeSai himself headed the search party, which was still active to this day, even though the woman they searched for no longer existed; she was now a shell of her former self, a beast like DeSai. Now they sought many more people who walked out their doors, never to be seen again. By the time the town realized what was happening and that DeSai himself was to blame for the disappearances, it was too late. He took to hiding, and they still had no idea where his sanctuary was. People continued to disappear, families were torn apart, and Manuel's men continued to hunt, not only for DeSai but for each of his victims who had become like him: bloodsucking monsters.

With one hand Jasso began to roll tobacco into a wrap for smoking, taking the aromatic shredded leaves from a pouch at his side. A twig snapped loudly behind him and, startled, he dropped the wrap filled with tobacco to the ground. Instinctively, he reached out to his right and grabbed the crude torch burning in a wooden holder. He held it out in front of him with his right hand and positioned his rifle firmly with his left. He swung the torch to get a look at what could have made the noise. Nothing was there.

He decided to walk the perimeter of the camp and began making rounds. His mind went to his wife, Danna, as he walked. How beautiful she had been, how gentle and kind. She had gone missing shortly after the first man; she had been one of the first to go. While he was sure she was still living, he knew she was no longer what she had once been, and this truth infuriated him to a murderous level.

They all discovered the truth about DeSai when one of the villagers observed him by the small pond outside of town. He was not alone; he was seen making love to the head councilman's wife, and she had been missing for months. This was immediately reported, and the ensuing investigation revealed that he had holed up all of the missing people in his home, and not only that, but they stayed of their own free will. Soon, one of the men that had disappeared was seen luring a teenaged girl to the outskirts of the village, and when the blacksmith attempted to intervene the girl was grabbed by him, and the man… took flight… with her in his arms.

Then they understood, and the specific hunt for Comte DeSai began. In the process, they began to find some of their missing loved ones, one at a time, and it became very clear that they were not the same. They were angry, evil, and violent. They would fight to remain under DeSai's roof, and under his control. Soon it was obvious: the monster intended to enslave the entire village, one person at a time. Jasso and his team of hunters would kill anyone who was one of DeSai's minions, regardless of who they had been in their previous life.

But it would never stop until they captured and killed DeSai himself.

All was clear around the camp, and Jasso returned to his post, replacing the torch in its holder. He exhaled then took his spot eyes ears alert with refreshed anger and grief from the thinking he had been doing. While he watched, he managed to roll a smoke and get it lit up. He took a long pull off the satisfying tobacco and felt his shoulders relax.

Wood snapped again behind him, but, this time, it was a much larger piece, and it emitted a loud 'crack!' rather than a snap. He jumped violently and swung around to face the direction where the noise came from. Someone, or something, was certainly out there, and he could feel its eyes boring into him.

"Who's there? Identify yourself immediately! I am armed!" Jasso strained to see in the darkness.

In front of him, from not more than ten feet, a calm, whispering, evil voice cut through the darkness.

"Manuel Jasso…"

Now he was more alert than ever. "Men, wake! DeSai is here!"

He heard the stirring of his men, their voices filled with anxiety as they pulled themselves from their slumber. "Where? Have you seen him?" Their sounds were overlapping and jumbled, and Manuel was not interested in responding. He took a step toward the voice.

"Show yourself!"

Suddenly something struck him in the side of the head with great force, knocking him to the side. He stumbled, but he did not fall. Jasso was a strong, lumbering man. He shook it off and began to look around him wildly.

There was nothing.

His men had taken up their arms and were beginning to mill about now. "Did you see that? Something hit Manuel! It is DeSai! He is here!" Torches were taken, and the men began searching in and around the campsite with great fervor. Jasso remained calm in his fury. He looked around carefully.

They would take the beast down this night, he would see to it.

The area around the campsite began to light up from

the torches the men carried, but nothing could be seen except the clearing and the trees surrounding it. Suddenly, one of the men screamed, and all heads jerked in his direction.

There stood DeSai. He held one of the men by the throat, and he had the large man up off the ground by a good eight inches. The Comte's long black hair, which was usually slicked back and gathered into a striking tail which hung down his back, was now unkempt. Running from these men had taken a toll on the man, but the look in his eyes contradicted this observation. They were rimmed with redness, and his mouth was a violent gash across his face which formed a dark smile. He was enjoying this; to him, it was not a hunt, it was a game.

Jasso started toward the once respected animal but stopped dead when he became aware that the man DeSai was holding was struggling for his life. The Comte had begun squeezing tighter, and the hunter could not breathe. Even in the dark, Jasso could see the color of his flesh taking on a deep shade of purple.

"Release him, DeSai! We want you; do not make this more difficult than it has to be. We will be victorious." Jasso kept his voice calm and steady; he would not appear afraid to this demon. It would only fuel him.

Comte Cyril DeSai chuckled and continued to squeeze. "This has been very entertaining for me, Manuel, but so has your beautiful wife. My, my, my, what a catch she has turned out to be!" He threw his head back and began to laugh with all his might, his hair blowing around his head in the wind.

Jasso did not even have to waste a second on thought. In the blink of an eye, he dropped his rifle and reached over his shoulder for an arrow to put on the bow he carried on his left side. In one deft movement, he loaded the arrow, raised it, and shot, all while DeSai indulged himself in his self-satisfied laughter.

The arrow struck him in the right side of his chest, its metal head piercing clean through him and coming out his back before stopping while still in his body. The Comte immediately dropped the gasping, sputtering hunter he had held by the neck, and he looked down at the arrow, surprise spreading over his face. He then looked up at Jasso.

"Ah, it seems I was not ready for you, Manuel…"

He bolted into the darkness in the direction opposite the forest and the trees. Manuel and his men did not hesitate; they began to run after him immediately. Jasso was reloading his bow as he ran, his rifle and the injured man forgotten behind him. As he ran, his thoughts went to the direction in which they were running; there was a cliff ahead, maybe seventy-five or one-hundred yards in front of them. He wanted to catch him and kill the monster with his bare hands first. He knew the Comte could fly, and he wanted to give him no chance to do this.

Suddenly the cliff came into view, and the sound of roaring ocean waters below grew very loud, indeed. Jasso and his men realized that Comte DeSai had not only stopped, but he had also bent over, his hands on his knees, and he was gasping for breath with great effort. The Comte was hurt; he was actually hurt somehow.

Manuel spoke. "So, you will do the noble thing and give yourself up, yes? You will see you err in what you have done and are doing? Or have I simply hindered your ability to fly away, evil bird?"

DeSai looked up at him, and still gasping, smiled. "There is no err in my ways; my ways are altogether perfect. What you construe as madness is truly the formation of my perfect kingdom…" His voice trailed off, and he took a step back, nearing the cliff's edge.

Manuel stepped toward him with the thought of getting to him quickly. The Comte's reply had done nothing but confirm his inability to fly off, even though he admitted nothing. He would have flown by now if he could.

Suddenly, DeSai stood erect and raised both of his arms straight out, as though he might take flight. Manuel rushed toward the man, reaching out to grab him when he was near enough. He nearly took hold of the Comte's lapel, but his fingers simply brushed the fabric. DeSai did not take flight. He fell backward off the cliff, eyes closed, ecstasy across his face. Jasso had to struggle with his balance to keep himself from going over. The other hunters were at his side in seconds, and together they watched as Comte Cyril DeSai plummeted into the murky, tumultuous depths below.

CHAPTER 2

Present Day

"Abby, you have to check out the ocean! I don't think I have ever seen anything so blue in my life." Patrick Gilliam turned slightly toward the slight blonde woman sitting next to him, his girlfriend, Abigail. He knew his suggestion for her to lean over him and look out the airplane window would go ignored, and that with great disgust. Abby was terrified of heights, and he liked to goad her into frustration. She was very cute when she was angry.

"Go screw yourself, Pat," she replied, crinkling her nose at him, but with playful eyes. She reached over and tousled his shaggy red hair before leaning her head back against the headrest on her seat and closing her eyes. Even imagining the ground below was enough to incite nausea in her stomach and vertigo before her eyes.

Across the aisle, sat their two companions, another pair of young lovers who loved to travel and Scuba dive when they weren't working. Abby shook off the fleeting sickness like a hot blanket and looked to the girl on her left.

"Candy, do you have any of those peanuts left? I

think my stomach needs something solid to settle it."
She gave Pat a slight elbow with the word 'settle,' just to
drive the point home. He smiled and continued to gaze
out the window at the clouds.

Candace and her boyfriend, Tim, both began to
rustle around in their seats and on their laps, both
knowing how Abby could get in the air. They were also
very familiar with Patrick's incessant teasing of his
chosen one, and Candy had taken to stashing something
extra just for this purpose.

"Did you get your hands on those peanuts, Tim?"
Tim Howell, who was still fumbling around for
sustenance to give Abby, dropped his hands into his lap
and looked at Candace Fredericks sheepishly, replying,
"I did…"

Candy shook her head and leaned to the right to get
a clear view of the aisle. "The flight attendant is coming
this way, but it will be about twenty minutes from the
looks of it. Do you want me to go get some from her,
Abby?"

Abigail Cayce shook her head and offered up a weak
smile. "Don't worry about it. I think I can hold out for
that long." She leaned back and closed her eyes again,
and Candy followed suit.

Tim turned to Candace. "Why don't you and Pat
switch seats, Candace? I'm all wound, and if all you're
going to do is snooze that's fine, but why make me sit
here and twiddle my thumbs?"

"You know as well as I do that Pat will never give
up a window seat to sit on the elbow-bumping aisle,

Tim." She shook her head, keeping her fond gaze on his chiseled features. She loved to Scuba dive, but she knew exactly why she was looking forward to landing, and it had nothing to do with the water, at least not initially.

"I'll give him mine, and I'll sit on the aisle then," he replied. He leaned over Candy. "Pat, come sit over here so these two sleepyheads can rest. You can have my seat if you insist on the window, dude, but I can't handle having no one to talk to."

Pat's eyes lit up; he was as bored with their travel partners as Tim. "Sure, man! Come on Candy, switch up." Pat was on his feet before he had even completed his sentence, and Abby was turning her knees out to allow him easy passage without even opening her eyes.

The two gathered their respective possessions and swapped seats. By the time they were settled in, Candy was pretty riled up and wide awake once again. The flight attendant had made progress to the tune of four sets of seats; she would stay awake to restock on peanuts and get herself a cold can of beer.

"Abby, when the attendant comes do you want a drink also? Might as well fuel up on something; we have another three hours or so to go." Candy kept her eyes on her friend, who looked a bit pale. How could she do this to herself time and time again? Well, she understood, really. There was nothing in the world like a Scuba diving venture.

Abigail opened one eye and turned her head slightly toward Candy. "Just peanuts and a bottle of water, thanks. If I have a drink, I'll puke for sure. Can I use your sleeping mask? Between the light and my slight headache, I just want to sleep. I don't want to deal with anything."

Candy fetched the item from her lap and put it on Abby herself. Then she got out her tablet and began to fiddle around with it to occupy her time. It never took long to get to their Scuba trips, but it was best to occupy one's time fully. She could hardly wait to get there. They would be diving in an area which was new to all of them, right off the coast of La Ceiba, Honduras. She had planned the trip herself and had done extensive research into the area's diving. It promised to be an experience none of them would soon forget.

Across the aisle, the guys had swapped out their seats quickly and efficiently, and Pat was already glued to the window, staring at the skyline. "Don't tell me I still don't have anyone to talk to, bud," Tim said to the back of his head. "If that was the case, I could have kept Candy over here; she smells a lot better than you do."

Pat threw his head back and laughed pretty loudly for an airplane passenger; a couple of heads from the seats in front of them turned, rising a bit above their headrests to make a point about the noise. "Sorry," said Pat, just as loudly. Shushing sounds began to accompany the glares. He looked over at Tim. "Nobody has a sense of humor anymore, man. Nobody." The two grinned at each other, and Pat settled back in. "So what do you know about the diving at La Ceiba? Has Candy given you any good info?"

Tim shook his head. "I don't think she really knows. Some girlfriend of hers from the gym recommended it, and she did a bunch of research on the area and the diving there. All she told me was that it was going to be great, but isn't it great every time?"

Pat nodded. "I think so, but, at least we'll get to see some new stuff down there. I was getting a bit sick of Hawaii and Mexico. Hope they party hard in Honduras."

They went into silence then. The attendant was only a couple of rows away, and the three who were awake had begun to straighten out exactly what they wanted from her in their minds: three cold beers, and as many bags of peanuts as she would 'shell' out.

In ten minutes, they had their provisions in their possession and their tray tables down, with the exception of a lightly snoring Abby. Tim turned to Pat. "One of these times, you are going to have to let that chick try to enjoy her flight, dude." They both broke into laughter, which caused a burst of hushes from the front of the cabin. Every time they flew, Pat managed to rile his girl up to the point of physical sickness; thus far, she had not made her infamous run to the facilities. Tim was glad he had lured his friend over to sit with him. It wasn't that long of a flight; he should let her sleep if she were able.

He looked over at Candy; she was preoccupied with her tablet. Pat was all but stuck to the window. He sighed and stood to get the latest copy of 'Scuba Diver' out of his carry-on bag over his head. If you can't beat them, join them.

The rest of their flight was uneventful, even peaceful, and before they knew it, it was time to wake Abby and begin getting their things together for landing and disembarking. The pilot came over the intercom and gave the obligatory speech about how grateful the airline was that they were chosen for this flight, and how they all hope to be chosen again, yadda, yadda, yadda. Before any of the four Scuba enthusiasts knew what was going on, they were walking toward the baggage carousel inside of the airport.

"That was a lot faster than some of our flights, it seemed," said Abby, as they stood watching for their bags. "Why is that, do you think?" Pat spoke up like lightning. "Because you weren't barfing every five minutes." He and Tim broke into obnoxious laughter, inciting the two thoroughly disgusted young ladies to shake their heads. Candy responded with a simple, "You're a couple of idiots."

Bags in hand, the troop headed to the front of the airport and stepped out into the hot, bright sunlight. Taxis were lined up at the entrance, with a few of them already loaded with passengers. Candy, always the one to take control, headed to an empty cab, leaving it to the others to follow at will. She leaned in the window and spoke to the driver. "Estrellas Cinco?" She spoke the name of the hotel fluently, and the driver responded with, "Sure. How many?"

Candy smiled. "Four of us, plus our bags. Is that

cool?"

"Of course," he replied. "One can take the front, no problem." He got out of the cab and walked to the rear to store their luggage in the trunk for the drive. The four climbed into the cab and got situated.

Pat was already glued to the window, but he spoke first. "How far is the hotel from here, Candy?"

She grabbed a small spiral notebook from her purse and flipped through the pages. "Supposedly about twenty miles; of course, we have to consider traffic, and we don't know this area so I would guess it will take us about an hour. If we over-estimate, we won't be disappointed, right?"

Tim groaned from the front seat; his girlfriend was forever the optimist. Sometimes he wished she would just lay it on the line and say she didn't know, but he had adjusted well to the fact that this would likely never happen, so he simply shook his head and smiled.

They wound up stuck in traffic twice, and on two different thoroughfares. The heat was nearly unbearable, and there was no air-conditioning in their cab. The only music on the radio was in Spanish, and Candy was the only one who understood it, and even the ever-cheerful Pat was ready to burst with frustration from the full bladder he had neglected to empty before leaving the airport. Their hotel was a much welcome sight.

∞

Estrellas Cinco, which meant 'five stars,' was anything but. It wasn't that bad, but when they entered the tiny lobby, they were quickly disappointed. Dusty plastic plants adorned each corner, and wicker furniture with dirty pads sat unused. There was a small desk which was something a school principal might use, and there was no air-conditioning. A box fan, aimed only at the clerk's desk, circulated the stifling air. Abby, Tim, and Pat fixed their eyes on Candy, who looked at them innocently and asked, "What?"

She reached out and tapped the bell on the desk, and within seconds a small mustachioed man appeared from a door situated in a small hallway. "Buenos Dias! Americanos?"

Abby spoke up. "Si."

"Good, good! I speak English. You have a reservation?" He replied in broken English. His smile was plastered to his face, and his eyes were lit up with eagerness.

Candy began to dig in her bag for her notebook with their confirmation numbers in it. "Yes, we do, let me just get the numbers out for you."

"That is fine, Senorita, but your name will be enough if you please."

She sighed with relief. "We have two rooms, two adults in each, and they are under the name Candace Fredericks. You will need my identification, I assume?"

"Your passport will be all I need to see." He began going through a hard-cover notebook, running his finger down the lines on the page. "Ah, Fredericks, four adults. Yes. I found it." He looked up and reached for Candy's passport, which she was already holding out for him to take. He opened it, looked it over, looked at her, and then smiled and returned the booklet. "Gracias, Senorita." With that, he began to enter information into the ancient desktop computer before him, and after a few moments, he looked back at Candy. "That will be a five-day, five-night stay at forty American dollars per room per night. The total will be four-hundred, seventy-five American dollars, which we do not take. Do you have 'lempira'?"

Candy had taken the time to conduct a currency exchange at the airport. She nodded and smiled at him while her friends looked at each other with grateful eyes; there was a reason they let her take charge.

"Then that will be ten-thousand, four-hundred forty-two lempira, please." The man's plastic smile remained on his face as Candy fetched the funds from her purse and paid for the rooms. Soon they were following the man, whose name tag identified him as Javier, down a hall as he pushed a rickety cart with their bags and led them to their rooms.

∞

The rooms were much better than the lobby had led them to believe. Air-conditioning pumped into them freely. They were spacious and attractively furnished, even offering a small refrigerator and wet bar in each one, though neither was abundantly stocked. The four divers began to unpack their gear and clothing and get themselves settled in.

Once finished, Abby walked out onto a small terrace which overlooked a small portion of the beach. Candy had done well once again. The beach was clean and beautiful; the water was a dazzling shade of blue, and it captured the rays of the sun like a blanket would catch strewn diamonds. It was intensely inviting. Tomorrow they would venture into the waters and see sites they had not viewed before. But until then, it was time to eat and party a bit; she turned and went back into the room she would share with Pat. "Are you done yet? I'm starved! Let's find the other two and eat."

CHAPTER 3

The crew walked up the hall in the direction of the stagnant little lobby. "I'm not exactly sure, but I think this place has a small café in it, though I don't know where it would be. It didn't look like it could, but that was one of the reasons I chose it." Candy held Tim's hand as she spoke, and squeezed it gently at the end of her sentence. They looked at each other, and she blushed slightly and smiled. They had pulled off a 'quickie' when they were supposed to be unpacking, but it was all she had thought about during the flight; their clothes could wait.

When they got to the lobby, Abby rang the desk bell, and Javier flew from the same door as before. "I can help you?"

"Yes, we thought there might be a café here where we can eat and have a drink, maybe even a bar with a grill?" Abby looked at the man hopefully, her stomach almost audible with its growling.

Javier's smile grew even broader if that was possible. "Ah, yes, yes, Si! Follow me, please!" He turned on his heel and headed back for the door which he had emerged from. They looked at each other skeptically and followed him.

They no sooner crossed the threshold of the door than they saw what had been occupying Javier. The door led to no more than a tiny room with a soda machine. Next to that was a large metal and glass swinging door, which he pushed and then held so they could enter. Spanish music could suddenly be heard, and bar signs adorned the walls of the room inside. A long bar with a haggard looking woman tending it was on the left, and a number of tables and chairs were situated on the floor of the room, each with napkin dispensers, salt and pepper, and bottles of hot sauce.

Candy smiled at Javier. "They serve food?"

"Si, Senorita! The very best in La Ceiba!" Candy doubted this but was willing to give it a go. They chose a table and sat down, getting as comfortable as possible in the hard, wooden chairs. The barmaid walked up to them and passed out laminated placards measuring about eight by fourteen inches: menus.

In broken English, she spoke to them, "I will take drinks, then come back for food."

Each of them proceeded to order a cold beer, and as she turned away, they placed their focus on their menus. "I don't read Spanish or whatever it is. Candy, I need your help." Pat seemed to be a bit edgy; he needed to eat.

"Fine. Let me choose, and then I will help whoever needs me, okay?" She took a long drink from her bottled beer and went back to her menu.

Within ten minutes she had chosen her fare, and she

had helped the others to do the same. They would keep it simple: baleada (balley-AH-da) similar to a Burrito, steak, rice, beans, and fried plantains all around. Just the thing they expected. Abby motioned for the barmaid, and they put their orders in. Finally, they could settle back and relax. They chatted comfortably about the initial dive they would make the next day, all of them excited about the new underwater frontier they would experience. When their food came, they ate mostly in silence, with just a few scattered words and sentences spoken between bites, and when they were finished they retired to their rooms, and each fell into an exhausted sleep.

∞

Patrick Gilliam slept hard if not soundly. His sleep was filled with disturbing, unexplainable dreams…

He was camping in a clearing in the middle of the forest with strangers. He sat on his bedding and looked around at all of the men sleeping around him. Why was he camping with a bunch of Honduran-looking dudes? Where was Tim?

He then noticed a man standing by a pole with a torch attached. He was staring around in the darkness, smoking what appeared to be a joint. Maybe he would share. Patrick spoke to the man, "Hey, you feel like passing that?"

The man's head jerked around, and he made eye contact with Pat. He drew deeply on the 'joint,' then dropped it to the ground and stepped on it. Pat watched in disbelief; how rude!

The man spoke to him in Spanish; Pat understood him, though he was clearly aware that he could not speak much Spanish at all. "When he comes, he can have you first. You are the beginning of the end."

"What the heck are you talking about man? Who, the cops? All I wanted was a hit, jeez, I'm sorry I asked."

The man smiled a grim, pained smile and shook his head. "He will have you first. You are powerless… we are all powerless."

Pat noticed a bruise along the side of the man's face in the firelight. Just as he opened his mouth to ask the man what happened to him, another man approached from the shadows and stepped into the light, standing next to the one with the bruise. His face was purple and bloated, and even in the dim light, Pat could see a deep black bruise around his throat.

He turned to the first and said, "Yes, DeSai will take him. He is good enough." He then turned to Pat and walked up to him. Looking him in the eye, he spoke directly to him, "This visit is not your own. You were all chosen for the beginning. Go home. Now… while you still have time…"

Patrick sat up straight in the bed, the sheets, which were twisted around his legs and torso, soaked with his sweat. He breathed heavily, gulping in the fresh air, along with the reality which now encompassed him. Honduras. He was in Honduras.

He turned to his right to confirm, and upon seeing Abby sleeping soundly next to him, he breathed a great sigh of relief. What the heck kind of dream was that? He had never really dreamed such a clear dream which involved characters he had never encountered before in his life.

He swung his legs over the side of the bed and walked into the bathroom to relieve himself and get a drink of water. When he was finished, he returned to the bed and settled in next to Abby, wrapping his arms around her and snuggling her. She moaned and snuggled him back in her sleep. The dream had all but faded now, and he closed his eyes. In minutes, he was sleeping soundly once again.

R.W.K. Clark

CHAPTER 4

The new day brought the sun, and with it, the suffocating heat. Candace rose before the others and, leaving a note for Tim, went down to the bar and grille. It was open, but the bar was unattended. Instead, there was a single waitress, and a man working in the kitchen behind the bar. She sat at the same table they had used the evening before and placed an order for pastelitos (fried Honduran meat empanadas), and coffee, which she sipped while her food cooked.

They were to be at the Scuba company by eleven; it was only eight now. She had plenty of time to sit and enjoy the peace and quiet of the morning. Adventure and excitement would come soon enough. She watched a man and woman talk outside through a window near her table. They gazed romantically into each other's eyes, and it made her smile.

As she watched them, their expressions changed. Suddenly, the man looked up and appeared to look her directly in the eyes; the woman turned and did the same. They held the stares, as did Candy. Their eyes held no malice, but they did hold fear, and it was enough to send a jolt up her spine.

Right then, the waitress brought her plate; Candace turned and looked at the steaming food. "Bueno," she nodded to the woman, who curtly nodded back before filling her coffee and walking curtly away. Candy turned back to the window, but the couple was gone.

She found she was no longer very hungry, but she picked at her food as best she could. She had one more coffee when she was finished, and as she sat and obsessed on the couple outside, her friends came into the café to join her.

"Always the early riser, our Candy," began Abby, who took a chair next to her. The men sat across from their girls, respectively, and Candace breathed a sigh of relief that she was no longer alone with her thoughts in this creepy place.

She smiled broadly, offering her grin to each one of them individually. "Good morning! Are we all ready to get wet today?"

They nodded enthusiastically, almost in unison. Tim stood slightly and leaned over the table, planting a kiss in the middle of her forehead. "How did you sleep, love?"

"Deeply. How about you two?" Abby nodded, but Patrick just gave a lame sort of smile.

"I tossed a bit, but I think it was just the new place. You know, we've never been here before. Tonight will be better after I'm worn out from the day." Patrick put his focus on twisting his napkin between his fingers and managed to change the subject by waving at the waitress, who made her way over with three cups and the coffee pot.

The three joiners ordered their food off the cuff and began to enjoy their coffee, getting woke up for the day's adventures. In no time their food was ready, and they ate in silence, knowing that they needed to get their gear gathered and find a cab to take them to the Scuba guide who would accompany them on their dive. Being late simply was not an option. Between suiting up, safety checks, and getting to know their guide, it was best to be early.

∞

At ten forty-five, the four of them arrived at 'Scuba Adventura,' a guide company which came highly recommended by Candy's boss, Mark Abrams. He said some of the best diving he had ever experienced was in Honduras, and led by the people there, so they had been the go-to when it came time to plan this trip.

Their guide was named Rodrigo, and he had fifteen solid years-experience with this company. While they geared up, they chatted and got to know each other better, and this continued even into their equipment checks and safety reviews. By the time they got on the boat and headed out, the team was more than ready to get the diving underway.

After about thirty minutes of boating, Rodrigo slowed the boat near the foot of a massive cliff. He stated in broken English. "Here looks like a good spot. A new area for me, but look very nice for good dive." All four nodded in reply and prepared to go in as he stopped and secured their vessel.

The dive itself went smoothly, and they began their underwater exploration with great avidity. They had paired off, each couple together, but they stayed in close proximity to each other, so they were able to share their discoveries. Candy always had her camera, and she loved to get as many good shots of the beauty of the ocean as she could.

The sea life was outstanding, as were the plants and variety of shells they saw. Brilliant colors filled their vision, and they eagerly shared all they saw with each other. Time passed quickly though, and Tim, who usually watched their air gauges obsessively, finally nudged Candy to signal that they had about twenty minutes left. She nodded, and the two proceeded to swim over to Pat and Abby to let them know.

They no sooner reached their companions when Pat began to signal to his left with his hand. The other three looked in that direction to see the mouth of an underwater cave. Tim tapped his wrist, letting Pat know that time was ticking quickly, and Pat responded by motioning that he just wanted to take a quick peek at the site. All four proceeded to the opening in the side of the cliff.

They swam into it cautiously, and the first thing they all took note of was its vast size; it seemed to go on forever. It was getting darker, and there was no end in sight. They all stopped and treaded water, looking at each other. Candy shook her head to say they needed to hit the surface.

When the four were back in the boat with Rodrigo,

they began to take off their gear. As soon as communication was possible, Tim spoke.

"How cool was that?" His eyes were lit up like a kid in a candy store.

Pat nodded passionately. "I know, right? I want to go back tomorrow. What do you two think?" He looked at both girls expectantly.

Candy responded, "I'm game. We'll bring some more supplies so we can explore it deeper. You know, better flashlights and the like."

"I'm excited, too. It's going to be a blast!" Abby chimed in.

Rodrigo fired up the vessel as the group told him what they had discovered, and they invited him to join them. He responded with much less enthusiasm than they anticipated for a seasoned Scuba guide. "I will bring you, but I will remain in the boat again. I have not been feeling myself." He sped up the motor and took off like a shot, turning away from the young divers and focusing on the water. Tim and Candy looked at each other, both of them raising their eyebrows; his behavior seemed a bit odd to them. Shifty, even.

They were back at the hotel by five, and after showering and dressing, they met up in the lobby to decide their next move. "Let's cab it to La Ceiba and find another restaurant. I'm ready to enjoy a night out and tour a bit." Tim Howell smiled and continued. "Maybe see some sites that are above sea level, you know?"

R.W.K. Clark

CHAPTER 5

The city proved to be colorful and exciting, with very energetic nightlife. The group started by taking in the sites they could, then around eight decided to pick a restaurant and have some supper.

They settled on a recommendation of one of the locals, the Golden Space, and while it proved a bit spendy, it was well worth it. The food was magnificent, and the drinks were just what they needed to relax and enjoy the evening together in the new city.

Regardless of their fun, they all were thinking about the cave. While none of them voiced the nagging thoughts, they were there nonetheless, strangely so.

At one point, Abby even grew frustrated with herself because thoughts of tomorrow's dive continued to distract her from the conversation at hand. All of them were plagued by them, and by eleven, they were hopping in another cab and heading back to their hotel and to their beds.

∞

Restful sleep evaded all of them. Each tossed and turned, dozing for brief periods. They all knew how important a good night's sleep would be to a successful dive, so they continued to try to get some shut eye. Pat couldn't seem to shake the spotty memories of the dream he had the night before, and none of them could put the cave out of their minds. It seemed to beckon to them all.

Candy finally fell into a fitful sleep around two in the morning, the soft snores Tim was putting out seeming to lull her off. From the moment she began to truly sleep, she began to dream, and nothing was settling about the visions going on in her mind.

She was underwater, Scuba diving in full gear. Her friends were with her, but they swam a good distance ahead of her, as though she were not even there. She struggled to catch them, but no matter how fast she swam, she could not close the gap between them. Why weren't they paying attention?

The water was dark and murky, and as she observed this, she took note of even deeper darkness up ahead. It was the mouth of the cave in the side of the cliff. Oh, yes! They were going to explore it today! She felt her own excitement, and with it, she felt a discomforting dread. She continued to swim forward, trying her best to catch up to the others.

They entered the cave, and though none of them had flashlights, her vision was clear in the murky water. Once she was in the cave, she looked behind her; the entrance was gone. There was nothing but solid rock. Her mind could not wrap around it, and her dread deepened, but she pushed it away and continued on.

The darkness deepened, but it did not affect her

ability to see in the slightest. The water she swam in was getting red, a deep shade of crimson. She wanted to turn around and leave; the others were not even paying her any mind. She turned and began to swim back in the direction she came from, but there was no entrance to be found. She continued to swim along the rock wall of the cave, back and forth. Nothing! Panic rose up in her throat, and she looked down at her air gauge. Only three minutes of air left! She looked frantically around for her friends, but she was alone in the blood red ocean, in the darkness, in the cave with no way out.

She woke to Tim shaking her. "Candy! Wake up! You're dreaming!" She was kicking and flailing her arms violently, still trying to swim. As she gained consciousness, she took a deep gasp of air into her lungs. She had been holding her breath.

"Oh! Oh, my, Tim! I had a terrible nightmare!" She began to cry immediately and uncontrollably. He held her and let the sobs run their course, comforting her and rocking her back and forth. Once the bout passed, she pried herself from his embrace and went into the bathroom, looking at the clock as she went; it was six-thirty in the morning.

Once in the bathroom, Candy looked in the mirror at her reflection. She looked haggard, even worn. What the heck was that dream, anyway? She turned the tap on and waited for the water to warm before cupping some into her hands and splashing it onto her face. As she brushed her teeth, the dream finally began to fade, but as she emerged from the bathroom to dress she remembered that they would be exploring the cave they found the day before, and tingle of dread filled her stomach and ran up her back and neck.

This is foolishness, she thought to herself. How many Scuba explorations had she and her friends been on together? She had never been one to balk at the unknown; if anything she faced these things with gusto and a sense of vendetta. Now she found herself balking at the fact that they would enter that dark space. She pushed the silly thoughts from her mind and smiled at Tim, who sat cross-legged on the bed looking at her expectantly.

"Are you okay?" The look on his face expressed deep concern, as did the tone of his voice. "You were really freaking out, and in your sleep, too. I've never seen anything like that."

She smiled as she pulled a pair of jeans on. "I'm fine. Just a freaky dream is all it was. You've had nightmares, you know what I mean."

He nodded in return and rose to dress as well. "Wanna go down for coffee since we're up? Then we can start to get our things together for today's dive. I'm excited about it! Wonder how deep that cave goes, anyway. It looked to me like it has a lot of potential, I tell ya!"

"Sure, sounds good," Candy replied. "Actually, that's what my dream was about…"

He turned his attention to her as he buttoned up his shirt. "What, the cave?"

"Yeah. The cave. We were all on the dive, and we

were swimming into it, and... and... well, I guess I lost you guys and couldn't find my way out. I was running out of air and couldn't breathe." She didn't look at him as she explained. She was afraid her eyes would give away her deep apprehension.

Tim walked up behind her and put his arms around her. "You know I would never let you out of my sight down there, don't you?"

Candy nodded and turned to him, wrapping her arms around him and returning his embrace. "Yeah. I know." She smiled and looked into his eyes. "Now let's go get that coffee."

∞

The two ate while in the café, and they sat and talked about whatever came to mind, chatting idly, their words having no real substance. By eight-thirty, they decided to go track down their sidekicks, who hadn't made an appearance as of yet.

The two would need to grab a bite, and both Tim and Candy wanted to make sure they had some of the extra supplies they would need to swim deeper into the cave. They were going to meet up with Rodrigo at eleven-thirty, so now was the time to get things moving.

∞

Rodrigo was packing their boat with the equipment needed for the dive. "So, you want to go back to the same spot as yesterday?" "You going into the cave?"

Pat was already on the boat. "Yep! Have you changed your mind? Are you going to join us?"

"No, no, no," Rodrigo replied. "I wait up here for you, but I will get you closer to the cliff side. You have things you need to explore longer? I get you anything before we leave?"

All four of them shook their heads in response, with only Abby giving him a 'no.' Soon enough, they were all in the boat, full air tanks and gear ready to go. There was a tangible sense of emotion in the air. For Tim and Abby, it was excitement which emanated from them. For both Candy and Pat, it was something more sinister.

They arrived at their spot much faster than the day before, or so it seemed to the crew, and in no time, the four of them were in the depths, swimming toward the cave. It had come into view almost immediately once they were in the water; Rodrigo had done an outstanding job of getting them back where they were before, almost as if he knew exactly where to go to get them closer to the cave. Tim was grateful to have him as their guide; he seemed to be one of the best they had ever had, if not the most strange and distant.

The group entered the cave, making sure to stay together. They had brought plenty of lights, each bearing their own bright source. Once again Candy had her trusty camera in hand, and they had plenty of air which would allow them to explore to their hearts' content.

As they swam into the darkness, the cave seemed to get narrow in some places, threatening to end, but it always seemed to change its mind and get wider before continuing on. There were no plants, and there was no sea life worthy of photographing, so they continued on. About fifteen minutes in, Tim slowed; the cave did indeed appear to end just up ahead. He turned to the others to find out what they wanted to do, and that was when his eye caught another narrow entrance. No, the cave would not end here. He nodded at them, and they all made their way toward it with him in the lead.

This was a much narrower passage, and as he entered with the others in the water behind him, he took immediate notice of the air pocket above. He turned slightly and held his hand out for them to slow down and wait. He needed to check this out, and there was not enough room for all of them to proceed together.

He entered the mouth of the outlet and swam upward toward what appeared to be surface water. He broke it, and immediately he was overwhelmed with what he saw. It was far more than an air pocket; this was a massive underground cave.

Tim shined his light around and tried to take in its magnitude. Finally, after processing their find, he went under and returned to his group, who treaded water waiting for him. He signaled to them that they would proceed, but single-file. That was all he revealed, and the others simply nodded in reply, ready to go.

He swam on, and once again broke the surface of the water leading to the cave. He placed his flashlight on its floor and hoisted himself up and out of the water, turning his attention to the five-foot by three-foot water hole he had just emerged from. Soon, Candy's head broke the water as well, and he reached out to take her hand and pull her to the floor of the cave.

Within minutes Pat and Abby joined them, and they were able to take their mouthpieces out and communicate. The air in the cave was fresh and cold, and it was not only breathable, but it was also invigorating. For a long moment, no one could even speak. They were all in awe at their find. Finally, Pat spoke and put everyone's thoughts into words perfectly.

"My Gosh."

The cave was so incredibly massive that it was overwhelming. Its walls climbed so high that their meager lights, which had seemed so powerful and sufficient up to this point, couldn't even illuminate any kind of ceiling overhead. Dampness clung to them until it was literally dripping, and it formed a small stream which seemed to flow around the base of the walls, running into the hole which they had emerged from. The rock walls of the cave were dark gray in color, and their texture was like any cave on Earth.

"Funny, but for all the wetness it doesn't smell damp in here. It smells more like a wet animal," said Abby, and the other three inhaled the cave's scent deeply at her prompting.

"You're right," replied Tim. "It smells kind of like a wet dog. I think this is the inside of that cliff, though. I doubt very highly there are any dogs in here."

Candy spoke up then. "Maybe there is another entrance." She shined her light at the others, one at a time. They all looked at each other, a mixture of confusion and wonder in their eyes.

"Let's look around," said Pat. He stood up awkwardly under the burden of his wetsuit, and the others did the same. "I really think we should all stick together, though. Who knows how big this place really is. If it is as big as the cliff itself, it could go on forever."

They began to walk, shining all four lights in front of them as they went. They were quiet, each listening for any sound that could be heard, but aside from their own footsteps, the cave was completely still. Their breathing seemed to scream out to them in their quiet surroundings.

Just as Pat had suggested, the cave went on and on, and it wasn't long before he spoke again. "Maybe we should stop for a minute." His voice had a slight tremor, and it was enough to capture the attention of the others right away.

"Are you okay, dude?" asked Tim.

Pat nodded. "Yeah, I just don't think we should go any further until we know. I mean, until we have a better plan that consists of more than just going forth blindly, you know?"

Candy's attention was completely captured. Forgotten was the dream that had woke her the night before, suffocating and screaming in her sleep. "I think we should camp here."

"We don't have the gear to camp here, Candy." Tim's voice sounded as though he thought his girlfriend had gone off the deep end. "I mean, it's a great idea and all, but once we dive and reach this place we will need to get our suits off and warm up; it's cold and wet in here. We have no bedding, no food. What are you thinking?"

She shook her head vigorously. "No, no. I don't mean tonight. We have another few days here, and we are scheduled to dive again tomorrow. We go back, gather some sufficient supplies. We pack them, so they don't get wet, and we dive and spend the night. That would give us a chance to really check this place out, and we would be back in plenty of time for our bodies to adjust from the dive before our flight home."

They were all silent as they considered her idea. "Well, I guess the four of us really wouldn't need much for a single night here, and each of us could tote our own gear on the dive," said Abby. "To be honest, I would love to see some more of this place. Who knows if anyone even knows it's here? We could discover some amazing things, and Candy could get some cool shots."

Without anyone giving confirmation, they all knew it was settled. Finally, Tim spoke. "Well, if that's the plan we should get back to Rodrigo and get our crap together. To be honest, I can barely wait."

They made their way back to the hole and got themselves ready for the dive and the swim back to the outside world. In no time at all, they were breaking the surface of the water, the sun hitting their faces and making them all squint against its violent attack on their eyes. The boat was about twenty yards away, and they made their way toward it, eager to board and get back to the hotel.

Once they were all back on the boat, Rodrigo went through his obligatory questioning in regard to their dive. "Did you go into the cave? I began to worry you run out of the air, you all gone so long."

Pat, who could barely contain himself, let the excited words fall out of his mouth. "Rodrigo, you wouldn't even believe it! Not only did we swim into the cave, but it led up into the cliff side. We were actually able to get out of the water, and we discovered another cave, a huge cave!"

Was Candy imagining things, or did Rodrigo's eyes flicker suspiciously away from Pat's face when he heard about the cave in the cliff? She pushed her paranoia out of her mind and carried on where Pat left off.

"Rodrigo, do you know about the cave in the cliff?"

Rodrigo was putting the gear into some compartments in the boat, and he answered her without looking at her. "No, no. I live here since I was born. You find something new down there." For someone who believed that he wasn't very excited.

Abby continued. "We are going to camp in there when we return on our dive tomorrow."

That caught the guide's attention, and his head turned sharply towards Abby. "Stay? In the cave you find?"

"Yes, Rodrigo, stay. When we come out tomorrow, we are going to spend the night in the cave. We will pay for the time you stay, or you can head back, and we will cover the cost for you to fetch us in the morning. Is there a problem?" Obviously, Tim had picked up on the guide's apprehension and strange behavior as well. He didn't take his eyes off Rodrigo's face as he spoke to him.

The guide began to rapidly shake his head. "No, no problem. I bring you back if you wish. I cannot stay overnight. I have a wife, you know? But I will retrieve you at whatever time you say the next morning. No problem." With that, he walked to the helm, started the boat, and took off from the spot like a shot.

Obviously, he wanted to get home to that wife of his fast.

CHAPTER 6

1796 Honduras

The freezing water hit him like shards of glass. Any other man would have died instantly, but not Cyril DeSai. Not only did the impact not faze him, but the water's temperature went virtually unfelt also. He smiled as he began to swim deeper and deeper into the water which rolled at the base of the cliff from which he had leaped.

He smiled as he gained speed. The arrow which had pierced his flesh stuck out of his body, waving back and forth with the movement of his strokes. He didn't feel that either, but had it struck him just a bit further to the right it would have been his end. That was why Cyril DeSai loved the darkness. It rendered his enemies powerless against him.

Ahead he saw the mouth of the cave, his cave. He always felt as if he were coming home when he saw it before him. After all, he had taken refuge in its hidden depths for centuries. As he neared the mouth of the cave, his heart began to settle. Even though it was dead, it still beat, keeping his body alive, and the unexpected turn of events caused by the arrow had sent a rush of uncontrollable palpitations through it. Fortunately for him, it was a feeling he greatly enjoyed.

He needed no light as he entered the dark cave; his eyes could see as clearly as if the sun were shining before him. He continued forward to the place that would lead him to his refuge, the inner cave. His speed was such that the water flushed quickly over his face, and in only seconds, he arrived. He broke the water's surface which led to the second cave, the cave above the water, and he did this with such force that his body shot up and out, and he landed with a feline's grace on the cave floor.

With a rapid shake of his head, he shed the beads of water which clung from the long mane that was his hair. Cyril looked around with satisfaction on his face. Home. It was here that he felt most comfortable, here that he could be who he truly was, and part of who he really was, was alone. Even with those he had made his followers, was he alone for they had no true understanding of him and his plight; his eternity of death that never stops cycling.

He began his stride into utter darkness, aiming for the heart of the cave. As he walked, he considered those he had acquired from the village in the recent past, his new family. They remained, but they were so new that they had no experience, much less sufficient knowledge regarding who they now were that they would soon be plucked off by the commoners. He never liked it when it came time to rid himself of those to protect himself. He could always move on to the next group of sheep and acquire new followers. Always and forever.

But even this fact didn't settle the black yearning in his soul, the very thing that drove him by nature to continue this charade. It had taken him over two centuries to analyze this unquenchable lust, but he did, indeed, finally understand his plight: the vampire soul within him, if one would call it a soul, was driven to discover its one eternal mate.

His cave's deep inner sanctum was a good distance from its mouth; the average human would be walking for an hour, but Cyril was able to reach it on foot in mere minutes. No one would ever reach it before he reached them, at least not if anyone ever found this place.

Cyril DeSai was enveloped in blackness. He turned his head to the right and blew a sharp breath. A large tallow candle sprung alight, and a full procession of candles followed suit one after another, all around the massive inner circumference of the inner sanctum. The cave lit up as though the sun itself were shining directly in its depths.

He didn't need the light, he wanted the light. It provided the only warmth in his never-ending life; a certain coziness he longed for but could never seem to obtain. Even to him, this seemed a silly and confusing thing to enjoy; he was a vampire after all. Regardless, he supplied himself with this comfort no matter where he found himself on this forsaken Earth.

He also had this area furnished; the walls and floor were all dry because he saw to it that the atmosphere within was maintained according to his desires. A single large chair, hand-carved from a single piece of oak and covered in red velvet, sat in the very center of the room, directly in the center of a hand-woven Spanish carpet. It was indeed good to be home.

When he got to the chair, he stopped abruptly. DeSai grasped his right hand firmly on the arrow that was planted through the middle of him. It had missed his heart by only a fraction, he knew; to hit his heart with such a thing would mean his death. He snapped off its butt end, and then reaching behind him, he grabbed it by the tip and pulled it completely out. His inner and outer flesh tingled with the sensation of instantaneous healing. It was intoxicating, and he closed his eyes and smiled.

There were benefits to being who he was.

He sat and made himself comfortable. Where to next? He pondered. He would simply move on, but no matter where he ended up, it was always temporary because they always came to a realization of what he was doing, and they always set out to destroy him at that point, but they would never succeed. He would simply leave, but not without having his fun with them, like he did earlier at the campsite with the 'hunters.' This thought made him smile.

But with all of this aside, Cyril DeSai knew, in his blackest heart, that this place, this sanctuary, would forever be his dwelling. He could find himself on the other side of this giant ball of mud they all called home, and he would still return here when they had their enlightened epiphanies. The only reason he had begun to take the villagers of Olanchito was that their nearness sprung a desire for their blood within him which he simply could no longer control. He had done it since they came, and he finally indulged his hunger (and his laziness) by purchasing the stead which his followers would call home, once he tasted them. Once he enticed them.

He settled in. Perhaps he would travel to Puerto Cortes and discover the delights they held for him, who he could 'take under his wing,' so to speak. This made him throw his head back and laugh aloud; indeed!

For now, he would enjoy the chilled warmth of home and tomorrow he would venture for the new place. The hunters of Olanchito would still look for him, and they would be on the lookout for many years to come, but he would not be found. He would move on and repeat the cycle which so plagued him. Change to the course would never be needed. There was not a thought in his mind of ending it.

He took a good look around his abode, and with what could only be described as a twisted flood of false love, he observed his children. The bat-like creatures hung from every possible nook and cranny, their eyes fixed on his every move, waiting patiently to carry out his bidding. Their look and smell made DeSai smile, and his chest swelled with the decay of pride.

He was nothing but an animal himself, and he would do what his nature demanded of him.

R.W.K. Clark

CHAPTER 7

Present Day

Tim, Pat, Candy, and Abby swam toward the cave eagerly, all of them laden with their personal camping supplies. They had chattered endlessly throughout the prior evening about their stay in this unknown place, and their talk had roused a strange passion that none of them had felt since they were kids. It was as though they were going to Disneyland for the night.

It didn't take long for them to reach the inner cave, and within only minutes of their arrival, they were all standing on the dry ground of the cave unpacking their gear and supplies. Soon, they were stripping themselves of their diving gear and pulling sweatpants and shirts on for warmth. Tim and Pat had both brought a bit of newspaper and a few small logs apiece in the packs; this would allow them to have an evening meal. The girls each had a bottle of wine. It would be a night to remember.

"Let's explore," began Pat. "Let's really check this place out and see what it's all about. I wonder if anyone other than us has ever been down here. Maybe we discovered something, well, brand new, you know?"

Candy couldn't help but smile and shake her head at his child-like excitement. "I'm game, and I'm ready."

The four set off with their flashlights in the direction which would lead them to the center of the cliff. During the initial stages of their walk, they gabbed and chatted about everything from Rodrigo and his strange attitude to their jobs. It was a relaxing time, and it felt good to see something new while enjoying each other's company.

Finally, Tim looked at his watch. "Guys, we have been walking for more than an hour. It's going on four o'clock, and my stomach is really starting to growl! It seems like this could go on forever." All four of them shined their lights ahead in a single, bright stream. There was no end in sight to the path they were on.

Candy turned to the other three. "You know, I thought that maybe we should keep this little jaunt close to our camp. After all, we have no idea where this leads or what we might find if and when we get there. The cave is cool and all, but it's not worth being utterly irresponsible, in my personal opinion."

Silence fell over the group, and finally, Abby spoke up. "Look, we have been fortunate enough to not only find this place but to get to camp here and spend some quality time together. I say we head back; by the time we get to the camp it will be nearing six, and we can have our dinner and some wine and settle in."

"Yeah, we can always plan an exclusive trip just to stay and exploring longer," Pat said. His voice seemed steady enough, but Tim was able to detect a flicker in his friend's eyes that seemed less than sure about proceeding.

"Are you okay, man?"

Pat nodded and turned to head back to the camp. "I'm fine. I guess I'm just hungry and tired."

Tim glanced at both of the girls before shrugging and nodding. "I'm ready. Let's head back, then."

The walk back consisted of far less talking than before. Each seemed deep in their own thoughts, and all that could be heard was the sound of their footsteps. The mood seemed to have shifted tangibly.

Pat was unsettled. He had been fine until they had all shone their lights up ahead. While there had been nothing to see, there was certainly something he felt, something… wrong. His arms had broken out in gooseflesh, and he had been the first to shine his light away. Something inside of him said that if he continued to look long enough something would appear, something none of them wanted to see.

Candy had felt it too, but to her, it was just a feeling of dread. There was no apparent reason for it, but it had been there, nonetheless, and she wanted to follow Pat back as soon as he had suggested it. She glanced at Tim as they walked. He seemed okay. Was she the only person who felt a bit disturbed? She assumed so and pushed the thoughts out of her head.

The fact of the matter was that all of them had felt it. Tim was pondering the feeling during the walk back as well, and Abby was trying to ignore the funny sinking feeling which had taken up residence in her gut.

Perhaps, she was more tired and hungry than she had initially thought.

By a quarter to six, they were back at the camp, and by six-thirty, they had a good little fire going, and Tim was heating a large can of beef stew right in the can. Each of them sported little paper cups filled with merlot, and by the time the stew was hot, they had all forgotten the mixture of thoughts and emotions they had experienced during their hike through the dark cave.

"Yummy!" Abby said. "I never thought I would say it, but this stew tastes downright gourmet. I was starved!"

The others nodded in agreement; they were all busy filling the void in the tired stomachs with the hot, hearty nourishment. The aroma of the stew filled the air around them, drifting into unknown parts.

Deep in the cave, in the direction they had been going during their explorations, a stirring began. The smell of the heated food began to rouse the life that resided in the cave's depths, and, literally, hundreds of eyes began to open all at once. Someone had come to visit…

Once the camp was cleaned up and the fire was out, the four friends adjusted their lanterns to illuminate their area correctly. Each poured another cup of wine and settled on their sleeping pallets comfortably; now was the time to talk.

"So, you think we should make plans just to come back here for our next trip?" Candy wanted to sound enthusiastic as if she were just as excited as they all had appeared to be, but her emotions didn't match the tone of her voice.

Abby nodded, sipping her wine. "Sure, I'm all for it. I just wish there was better light down here. It seems so damn creepy, and I guess the deeper we head into the darkness, the more spooked I get."

"Well, we would certainly want better light sources, if we are ever going to go any deeper," Tim replied. "I think the darkness appeared to be so ominous that it sort of repelled us." He chuckled at his choice of words.

Pat remained silent but nodded in agreement with all that was said. He wouldn't admit it, but when the time came to begin planning this trip they were talking about, he intended to come down with something… suddenly. He had absolutely no second thoughts about avoiding this place like the plague once they were out of here.

He drained his cup and snuggled down into the pallet. This caught Abby's attention, and she filled her own cup one final time before taking her place next to him. "Are you okay?"

"Yeah, just getting comfortable," replied Pat, winking at her. She smiled at him, finished her own wine, and dove under his covers with him.

"Well, I guess Candy and I ought to be able to figure out when we aren't needed anymore," Tim said with a smile. He looked over at his girl, and she smiled back knowingly. She was more than eager to take advantage of the sexual opportunity. Anything to get her mind off the nasty feeling in her gut and the oppressive atmosphere of the cave.

Tim reached over and dimmed their lantern. It would be much better if each couple could pretend the other wasn't there, not to mention easier to concentrate. He found Candy's face in the darkness and began to kiss her with passion. Regardless of the strange vibrations in the air, this was indeed something he would remember for a long time to come.

All four of the young people made love, but it was a bit stifled and stiff for Pat and for Candy. If Tim or Abby noticed the apprehension in their partners, they didn't let on; if anything it seemed to drive them. This proved to help the situation, but the lovemaking was brief, to say the least. Both Candy and Pat ended up faking their desired outcome before the four of them all fell into a fitful sleep.

∞

Tim was walking into the heart of the cave, his flashlight shining out in front of him brightly. He was thinking to himself that even though it was so bright, it did nothing for his vision. He could see nothing but the cave walls and pitch blackness.

Suddenly he heard a noise and stopped. What the heck was that? It sounded like a high pitched screech, and it sounded like it was far, far away. He stood in his tracks, staring into the nothingness before him, straining his ears to pick up any sound he could possibly hear.

Finally, he gave up; it must have been his imagination. He continued on.

There it was again, and this time he was sure it was a

screech! It had to be an animal, but what in the heck would be living down here? He turned to say something to the others, and it was then he realized he was alone in the cave.

It was then that he heard the flapping wings, and they were all around him. He began to shine his flashlight wildly around him, but he could see nothing. The ungodly flapping grew louder and louder until it was deafening. Then the screeching began to fill his ears as if it was inside of him.

He realized he was screeching. It was the sound of his very own screams…

R.W.K. Clark

CHAPTER 8

"Tim! Wake up!" Candy was shaking the man next to her with all the strength she could muster but to no avail. He was sitting bolt upright next to her, and his eyes were wide open and filled with panic. His screams echoed throughout the cave. He was terrified.

Suddenly both Pat and Abby were there, and all of them were attempting to jostle the petrified man back to consciousness. As quickly as the screaming had begun, it stopped, and Tim began to gulp in great breaths. "What the heck!"

"Are you okay, honey? What the heck were you dreaming about? You sounded like someone was killing you!" Candy had a frightened look on her face; something was very wrong down here.

Tim looked at his watch, pressing the light to illuminate its tiny screen. "Jeez. It's eight o'clock, you guys. Rodrigo is going to be up there waiting in a half hour. We need to suit up, pack up, and head up." He was covered in sweat, and his hair was damp and in complete disarray. He didn't take notice. He wanted to get the heck out of this cave; he wanted to skip the eighteen-hour waiting period for divers and get on the airplane home today.

The others all began to gather their belongings and get suited up for the swim back to the surface. As Abby loaded her pack, she glanced over at Pat, who was vigorously rubbing his neck with an open palm as he packed.

"What's wrong, Pat? Did you sleep on your neck wrong?" She thought that the cold, hard floor of the cave had taken its toll on her lover.

He continued to rub the area and shook his head. "No, I think I have a mosquito bite or something. It stings and itches."

Abby walked over to him with her flashlight and shined it on the spot. "Yep, it sure looks that way. It looks like the bugger got you twice. There are two little tiny prick marks right next to each other."

"I'll put some calamine on it when we get back to the hotel," Abby said. "We need to get going now."

The foursome finished packing up and took their dive, and within twenty minutes they were all breaking the surface of the water. Rodrigo was stationed only fifty feet away, waiting patiently for them. He helped each of them into the boat one by one, and soon they were headed back to the tour company, all of them eager to get into a taxi and begin to close the door on this trip.

As the boat cut through the water smoothly, Pat continued to rub his neck with the palm of his hand. He was thinking about the darkness in the pit of that cave, and he was thankful that they were riding in the boat with the sun shining on them.

∞

Once they were back at the hotel, the four all decided to spend their last night in La Ceiba with their mates alone in their rooms. It would be perfect and without having to keep things quiet, as their lovemaking in the cave.

Pat found his sexual appetite was at a peak. Abby could barely cross the room without his thoughts taking a dive straight south. The lust he felt in his body and soul was almost unbearable. He couldn't remember feeling a passion quite so strong, even as a growing young man. The four ate supper in the dreary café, having a few drinks as well, and then made their way to their rooms. Pat found he had no patience; he wanted to retire before their dessert had even made it to the table.

∞

"So, Abby, what do you have on your mind for this nice little evening with me?" He was leering at her, and his voice had taken on a syrupy quality that caught her attention immediately.

She turned to him and gave him a shy smile, her cheeks flushed with anticipation. "I don't know, sexy. What did you have in mind?"

That was all it took to get him moving. With the grace and speed of a cat, he crossed the room and swept her off the floor. She burst out laughing in surprise, but the look in his eye was filled with passion. He didn't even smile at her laughter.

He didn't take her to the bed; he spun around and laid her down on the floor in front of the television set. He proceeded to strip her naked, and none too slowly. At first, she felt a tinge of disappointment; she hoped the actual act wasn't as rushed like this. But she had nothing to worry about. As soon as she was naked, he gave her body a leisurely stare from head to toe, a smile creeping across his face. Then as fast as the wind, his head was between her legs, and he was not rushing; he was using his tongue and taking his sweet, sweet time.

Abby closed her eyes and threw her head back in ecstasy, her mouth open wide in pleasure. His tongue was moving in slow, torturous circles, and he was doing things with the fingers of his right hand that she had only heard about. This was not the first time Pat had bestowed this particular favor on her, but it was certainly the best.

She didn't know how much time even passed. All she was aware of was that she came so many times she lost count, and it didn't seem that he was anywhere near tiring out. Finally, she came for the very last time with a scream, and buried her hands in his hair and ground herself against his face, hips arched completely off the floor. Before she even knew what was happening, he was on her, and with a violent thrust he was inside her so deep she cried out from the surprise.

He held her to him and used his hands to hold her tightly at the shoulders, and he began to pound himself into her with urgency. She opened her eyes and saw that he was looking at her face, and he was smiling with the entertainment of watching her expressions as he took her as roughly as he ever had. As soon as they made eye contact, he gave her one final thrust and ground his hips against hers as he came. She could actually feel his penis pulsating inside of her.

He never even flinched, and he never took his eyes from hers.

They both slept right where they were on the floor, sweating and heaving in each other's arms. Neither even remembered falling to sleep.

∞

Tim and Candy enjoyed a couple of games of cribbage and some very typical lovemaking before falling asleep in their bed with the television tuned in softly to an old episode of 'Happy Days.' Right before drifting off, Tim thought briefly about his cave dream, and he knew he had enough of this place.

They were all ready to go home.

∞

"Tim, I need you to go down and settle the bill with the hotel clerk. Do you mind?" Candy was packing up her belongings, as he had been, but now he was finished, and he was perusing the channels on the television with the remote control. "We need to be out of here before eleven-thirty, and it's nine now, and none of us have eaten. It would really help."

Tim shut the TV off and stood, stretching his arms above his head to loosen up his lanky frame. "No prob.

I needed to get out of this room anyway." He came up behind her and planted a kiss on the back of her neck. "Where is the credit card?"

Candy turned and rifled through her purse briefly before turning back and handing the small rectangle of plastic over to him. "Will you stop in the café and have them make up four breakfasts to go? Oh, and some coffee too, please."

"Sure thing," he replied, and he winked at her as he left the room.

She hated packing to leave their trips. Not because she was so sick of the vacation itself, but because she always seemed to forget something in each and every hotel room they stayed in, and her obsessive-compulsive mind would drive her completely mad with worry. She began stacking clothes according to the wearer: Tim's things here, mine over here; repeat.

The phone jingled loudly, startling Candy into jumpiness. It continued its incessant ringing until she ran to it and picked up the receiver. "Hello?"

"Candy, it's Abby. Could you come to my room for a minute? I want to show you something." Her voice sounded a bit strange, almost afraid.

Candy didn't hesitate. "Sure thing. I'll be there in a sec." She plopped down the receiver and turned to head out the door. She didn't even knock when she arrived at Pat and Abby's room. The only thing on Candy's mind was getting her packing done, but her friend, of course, came first.

"What's going on?" She did want to get back to her

room and finish up her tasks.

Abby's eyes seemed riddled with worry. "Come in the bathroom. I want to show you something."

The two women headed in, and as soon as they got there, Abby pulled her long light brown hair up off her neck. "Will you look at this bug bite? It's tingly, and it itches a bit."

Candy leaned forward and squinted at the spot her friend directed her to. She saw two tiny puncture wounds, one right next to the other perfectly, just like Pat showed them in the cave.

"Maybe you got bit by something when Pat did?" Candy ran her index finger over the area on Abby's neck.

Abby shook her head. "That's what I thought at first, but Pat felt his bite right away. Mine wasn't here until I woke. Do you think it is some kind of bug that lives around these parts?"

"I don't know. It is kind of strange. What kind of bug bites in two different places every time? Should I search it on my smartphone?" Candy was at a loss. It was, indeed, strange.

Abby then began to nod. "Yeah, Candy. That would be good. I feel worried, and I don't even know why."

"I'll be right back," Candy told her, and she popped quickly over to her room and grabbed up her phone.

Once she was back, the two sat on the foot of the bed and Candy proceeded to begin doing a bit of research on the minute puncture marks on her friend's neck. Aside from horror fiction, the only information they could find pretty much pointed at a bug bite of some sort, but they couldn't pinpoint a specific insect species to attribute it to.

Finally, Candy stood and let out a big sigh. "Well, I don't think you are going to die," she said, smiling at Abby. "Finish packing and let's get to the airport. We'll all feel better when this vacation is behind us, I think."

Just then the door opened, and Pat walked in. His color seemed to be drained, giving him an almost ghostly pallor, but his eyes seemed very, very alive.

"Hello, ladies. What are the two of you up to?" Even his voice was off; the usually bumbling Pat now spoke with smooth confidence. Had he ever used the term 'ladies' in reference to a couple of females before in his life?

He walked up to candy and ran his hand through her hair. "You look good today," he said, holding her eyes in a mesmerizing gaze. Abby looked on without even flinching. While her mind thought the scene between her friend and her lover was a bit off, the rest of her seemed to tingle just from watching.

"What's going on with you, Pat?" Candy forced a chuckle, but her stomach was doing flip-flops. Was he drinking this early in the morning?

Her thoughts were quickly halted as he lowered his mouth quickly on to hers. She struggled against his kiss, even trying to break away, but he held her to him firmly with the single hand on the back of her head. Wow, could this guy kiss! Why wasn't Abby doing anything?

Soon she stopped fighting him altogether and began

to kiss him back. The entire time this was happening, her mind was going crazy, but she was powerless against his advances. She felt another set of hands stroking her back and sides, and she realized with curious horror that Abby was touching her as well.

The other woman's hands were soon under her shirt, stroking Candy's breasts through her bra. Her knees grew weak, and her legs turned to jelly. With one violent jerk, Abby tore Candy's shirt asunder, and it fell to the floor around her feet. None of this seemed real.

Pat stopped kissing her and gazed at her face as he reached behind her and unhooked her bra; it too fell to the floor, forgotten. He put his mouth on her nipple and swirled his tongue around it; his hand found its way under her skirt, and he began to stroke her through her light cotton panties. Her legs gave out, and she fell backward into Abby's arms. Abby slowly lowered her to the floor, and Pat's hand picked up its pace. She came within seconds of lying down.

For the next half-hour, Pat and Abby used her body lustfully, and together they brought her to climax over and over. She seemed to be in a cloud, and while she had no visual memories of the incident, she could remember every moment and every sensation they gave her. She slept, but only briefly, and when she woke she was clothed and on her own bed in her and Tim's room.

It was a dream; it had to be a dream.

Her things were completely packed and had been placed next to the door for pick-up. She rubbed her neck and quickly walked into the bathroom. She looked fine, but she had a different shirt on than the one she had been wearing when she went to Pat and Abby's room. It had been real.

The door to the room opened, and Tim walked in. "Are you coming? The cab is waiting, and everything is settled with the house. Time to go, babe."

"Yeah, yeah. I'm ready." She grabbed her purse from the end of the bed and looked around the room one last time. "Let's get the heck out of here."

CHAPTER 9

New York City, Present Day

Cliffside Winery hustled and bustled with busy employees, all focused on completing their tasks. There was much to do, after all, and there always was; Cliffside had become one of the premier wineries in the world. It produced every kind of wine imaginable, and each and every sample had come to be award-winning. There was never time to waste, as the orders continued to roll in constantly. Each and every person working there knew the importance of keeping the 'big man' happy.

The 'big man,' the boss, was Mr. Cyril DeSai. He introduced the world to his wares, and like a landslide, in the rain, Cliffside took off. That was twenty years ago, and in the time that had passed since, he solidified his position as a businessman and philanthropist in the States. He had eaten with presidents, and his wines could be found in every household in America. Coming here had been one of the smartest things DeSai had ever done.

Shirley Louis was Mr. DeSai's assistant, and she was all business. He was the most important person in the world to Shirley; he had literally taken her off the street and given her a future. She may be only twenty-eight years old, but she knew with a surety that she would retire a comfortable woman; DeSai made sure of that.

He was like a father to her.

She briskly rushed down the plushly carpeted hall to his massive office. It was easily the most beautiful office in the entire building, and DeSai's taste in more gothic décor only contributed to its mysterious lure. She loved to enter the great room and experience his presence. It was almost like being before ageless royalty. He kept the interior lighting very low, mostly using natural flame candles to illuminate things, but this only made it more special.

She tapped lightly on the hand-carved double-doors, and before she even pulled her hand away, she heard his heavily-accented voice tell her to enter.

"Mr. DeSai, you wanted me to let you know the details about flight 452 from Honduras. It will be landing at four o'clock tomorrow morning. Is there anything I can do regarding this? Do you have friends or family who will need transportation from the airport, or maybe a room?"

DeSai sat at his desk, his back to the young woman, but now he spun the high-back leather desk chair around and faced her. "No, no, Ms. Louis. Thank you for the update. That will be all." He steepled his fingers, placing the two index fingers under his chin, and he instantly went into deep thought.

Shirley nodded curtly. "I'll be at my desk if you need anything, sir." She softly closed the office doors and left him.

DeSai's eyes flickered and a smile formed on his face. His new family members would be home soon.

∞

Tim held Candy's bags while she dug through her oversized purse searching for the keys to her apartment. She was grumbling under her breath, even using curse words he had never heard her use before.

"I know I have asked you this many times, but are you sure you are feeling alright?" He felt a pang of apprehension in his stomach. He didn't care what she said, she was not herself, and she didn't look the greatest either.

She pulled her keys out and let her purse fall to the floor at her feet. "Finally, and for the last time, I'm fine, Tim! Jeez, do you have to be such a damn hen?" She inserted the key into the lock, then the next into another, and after a total of three were opened the door sprung open. "I'm just tired. I mean, we just got back, it's not even six in the morning, and you won't quit hacking on me. Please, just come in and get some shut-eye with me. That's all I need."

Tim warily kept his eyes on her as they entered the apartment. He took the bags to the bedroom; he had brought his up from the cab as well, hoping she would want him to stay. He wasn't thinking of sex, he thought she shouldn't be alone.

When he came back into the small living area, she was sitting on a stool at the bar which served as a divider between the common room and the tiny kitchen area. She was taking a corkscrew to a bottle of wine, and she was quite eager.

"Candy, it's practically dawn. What are you doing? Do you intend to get drunk before you even sleep?" He waited for her response, but all she did was look at him and roll her eyes.

"Instead of standing around asking stupid questions, why don't you help me with this? I just need to relax a bit before I turn in," she replied. She handed the bottle, with the corkscrew already embedded in the cork, over to Tim. He took it, staring at her with heavy apprehension.

He shifted his focus to the task at hand, and Candy went into the bathroom. She grabbed a pair of comfortable blue pajama pants and a matching t-shirt off the hook on the back of the door, and then looked in the mirror. Wow, she looked a wreck! Dark circles had formed under her eyes, and she seemed pale. Hopefully, she hadn't contracted some damn bug in Honduras.

She laid the pajamas on the sink's vanity and picked up her hairbrush and a hair tie out of a basket on the back of the toilet. She proceeded to brush her long hair, sweeping it up off her shoulders to put it in ponytails.

There they were: two tiny puncture wounds, the same bite marks Abby showed her. The same ones Pat had woke up with after their night in the cave.

She strained her neck to the side and leaned forward to get a better look. There was no mistaking what she saw, and while she felt no particular concern, she didn't want Tim to take notice of them. He was unusually nitpicky. She let her hair fall around her neck. Forget the ponytails.

She changed into her pajamas and meandered back into the living room, where Tim had already poured her a glass of wine. He also had the television on and was watching the early morning news. They were reporting on tours at a winery, Cliffside Wineries, to be exact. He glanced up at her and smiled.

"Better?"

She returned the grin. "Much. Thanks for opening that; I really need to get rid of my tension." She turned her attention to the television, where they were now interviewing the owner of the winery. His name, Cyril DeSai, was across the bottom of the screen.

Candy froze. She knew this man, and it was not from a passing meeting on the street. She knew him!

But how?

She tried to wrack her brain, but it seemed she could not keep her focus; she was entranced by the man on the screen, by the sound of his voice. When he looked into the camera, she could swear he was looking directly at her.

The interview wrapped up, but she still could not shake herself out of the reverie she found herself in. Her crotch had begun to tingle as she watched, and now it seemed it was on fire.

"Candy, are you okay? Did you fall asleep sitting up?" She pulled herself back to reality to see Tim leaning forward. He was looking at her, amused. She lifted her wine glass to her lips and drained it entirely, then she fixed her gaze on him again. Her lips curled into a seductive smile.

"No, no. I'm still here. Are you here?" She narrowed her eyes to match her smile, then licked her lips slightly for effect. Wow, was she in the mood to simply climb this man like a tree! Her mind shot to the 'dream' she had about Pat and Abby, and she became overwhelmed with wanton lust. She rose from her place on the sofa and crossed the room to Tim, removing her t-shirt as she went. Before she even reached him, she was completely naked.

It took no time for the pair to get going; they skipped the bedroom altogether. In the back of her mind, Candy thought that the floor seemed to be her thing lately. They kissed passionately while lying there, their bodies writhing against each other hungrily. His clothes were gone before he even realized what had happened. He put his focus on her breasts, licking and sucking her nipples, but she grabbed his head and brought it up to look her in the eye. She gave him a long, leisurely French kiss, then began to kiss his face. She gently kissed and licked at his cheek, his ear, his neck. With her eyes wide open, and with full intent, she bit him.

"Ouch! What the heck, Candy?" Tim jerked away from her, and his hand flew to his neck. He pulled his hand away and looked at the palm; two tiny smudges of fresh blood were visible there.

Candy's eyes grew wide, and she scooted away from

him, grabbing her pajama pants and using them to cover her breasts. "Sorry. I guess I lost control for a second." She reached for her t-shirt. "Did I hurt you that bad?"

He looked up at her and nodded. He looked totally freaked out. "I'm bleeding! What were you doing?" His erection was completely gone, and suddenly she didn't feel so enthusiastic either.

"I wasn't doing anything! I didn't mean to nip you so hard, I was just turned on I guess. I can see this little session is over," she replied. She stood and began to dress. "I'm just gonna go to bed. You can stay if you want."

Tim still had an incredulous expression on his face. Not only was she distant, but she was also completely detached. It was as if she wasn't even there. No, he wouldn't stay.

"I think I should just get home," he said, and he too began to dress. "I have to work tomorrow, and I need to unpack and all that." Once he was fully clothed, he approached her; she was back in her original position on the couch. He bent down and planted a kiss on her cheek. "Why don't you call me after you get some rest?"

Candy barely looked at him. She had the remote in her hand and turned the television on, simply responding, "Sure."

He turned the doorknob and stopped, turning back to his girlfriend. Her eyes were fixed on the TV screen.

"Love ya, Candy. Talk to you soon." He walked out and quietly closed the door behind him, rubbing his neck as he walked down the hall to the elevator.

R.W.K. Clark

CHAPTER 10

Candy Fredericks spent the next hour staring at the television without hearing a word that was being said. She was aware that she was doing this, but it was as if she had absolutely no power to do anything else. She should be asleep, but she simply didn't feel at all tired anymore.

Finally, she stood and made her way to her room and her bags. She ignored the need to unpack and walked to her dresser, where she chose a pair of faded skinny jeans and a cream-colored sweater. She dressed, slipped on a pair of loafers, grabbed her purse from the bed, and left.

She hailed a cab once she was outside. She had no idea where she was going, but she knew with certainty that she had to get there, wherever it was. She told the cabby to head north to the country.

He took off, and she simply stared out the window of the cab, waiting to discover her own destination.

∞

Pat Gilliam was sound asleep in the bed next to Abby Cayce. She was awake and had been since they lay down. She looked over at the alarm clock on her nightstand: seven-thirty in the morning. It was time to go.

She turned to her boyfriend and gently nudged him. Immediately his snoring stopped, and his eyes opened as though he hadn't even been asleep.

"We should go for a ride, Pat," she said simply. He nodded and turned over, swinging his legs off the bed to stand. The two dressed in silence then left the apartment. They, too, hailed down a cab, and Pat told their driver they were heading upstate; the driver obliged their demands, asking for no further information.

∞

Timothy Howell never even made it back to his apartment. He began walking, and after about forty-five minutes, he decided he wanted to take an impromptu tour of Cliffside Wineries up north. The TV had said that tours were offered every day from nine to five; if he took a taxi, he would arrive in time for the very first one of the day. Besides, he just wasn't tired anymore.

None of them knew it, but they were going home.

∞

Cyril DeSai sat in his throne-like office chair. It was seven-thirty in the morning, and he felt the first mental stirring in response to his call. The other three came like stair steps after that. He sat back, rocking slightly and resting his chin on his hands. Indeed, things were going to take off now. Soon, he would begin to re-establish himself, and it would be heaven. At least, as much heaven as a demon like DeSai would ever get.

There was a familiar light knocking at his doors. "Enter," he said with his thick accent and deep voice. Shirley Louis opened both doors.

"You called me, Sir," she began timidly.

DeSai smiled at his assistant. "Yes, my dear. I am expecting four visitors within the next couple of hours. Their names are Candace Fredericks, Timothy Howell, Abigail Cayce, and Patrick Gilliam. Be sure they are brought to me immediately upon their arrival."

"Absolutely, Mr. DeSai, as soon as they arrive." Ms. Louis was jotting their names in a steno pad as quickly as he spoke them. "Will there be anything else?"

"Thank you, Shirley, but not now." He smiled and stared deeply into her eyes; she always melted when he became so intense. Her knees almost began to visibly knock. She simply bowed slightly and backed out of the office, closing the double-doors as she left.

R.W.K. Clark

CHAPTER 11

DeSai smiled to himself and sat back in his chair. He had been waiting so long. This was everything he had wanted for literally hundreds of years; since the end of the last time, anyway. He had ached for those he had lost, ached with a deep yearning that had fought for its life. But he had won, and after a time it had faded. Slowly and patiently he had put his 'life' back together again. He had focused on what he needed and what he wanted: a family. His intense focus was finally paying off; they had arrived.

He was not aware of their arrival in La Ceiba until their fate was sealed. Once the first bite had taken place, he had felt the rush of their existence, and it had woken him out of a dead sleep, from the darkness of his crypt during the high noon hour. Yes, someone was in his lair. Someone had found his truth and decided to explore it, much to their own personal detriment. Initially, he thought it had been only a single soul, but his beautiful minions told him otherwise, and he became aware of the fact that there were actually four of them. They had all found his inner sanctum together. What a gift! With four he could begin his family much,

much faster than usual; with one it would take a very long time to build his kingdom. Four was far more than he would have ever dared ask for. Things would move along much, much faster this way.

He wanted to welcome them with open arms.

∞

Candy stood at the main gate at the visitors' entrance at Cliffside Wineries, her neck craned back so she could look at the sign. Her heart was fluttering in her chest, and even though her mind was confused as to why she was even here, something in her soul knew that the sum of her days would culminate today, at this place. She heard a car door behind her and turned around. It was a cab, and Abby and Pat were getting out. She looked at Abby and smiled without saying a word. No words were needed; they were home. None of them were surprised to see the other.

As the couple joined her on the sidewalk, yet another cab pulled up. Tim. After paying his driver he joined the other three, and in silence, they walked through the gate and made their way to the main entrance of the building. Even as Tim arrived, even as he tried to sort out his mental confusion, he felt a certain peace about all of it. None of them had yet associated their bites with the strange compelling they all felt; it was as if Honduras, and the subsequent occurrences, had never even happened. This was just another day.

Pat reached the main door first, and he opened it for the other three. There was a young woman seated at a desk typing furiously. She looked up, and her face immediately broke into a smile. She made eye contact with Abby first.

"Hello," she said warmly. "Are you four here for a meeting with Mr. DeSai?"

Abby nodded, even though she had no idea who 'Mr. DeSai' even was. "Yes," she replied. "Mr. DeSai."

"Good. He's expecting you. I'm his assistant, Shirley Louis. He'll be pleased to know you are here. Follow me." She began walking up a marble corridor, glancing behind her to make sure they were on her tapping heels.

The four didn't even look at each other, they simply followed her lead. The hallway was quite beautiful, adorned with art which ranged from traditionalist to contemporary. Sculptures were sitting atop gorgeously carved wooden pedestals; some of them were a bit morbid, but all were intricate and breathtaking. They featured dragons and demons with long, ravenous teeth. None of them even took notice of any of this.

After a brief elevator ride, Ms. Louis and her small group emerged and began walking down yet another hallway, which was decorated much the same way. The lighting was a bit dimmer, and each of them was thankful for this. The darker atmosphere seemed so calming; the light seemed a bit… painful.

They reach a set of massive double doors which stood ominously at the corridor's end. They seemed to dwarf the five people standing before them; it was all they could do just to take in their size and the ornate design which they adore. Candy sucked her breath in sharply. Yes, all things had led to this.

The assistant tapped lightly on the left door, her other hand grasping the handle as she did so. They all clearly heard the voice on the other side, even though it seemed to speak as softly as a light summer breeze. It was tantalizing.

"Enter."

Ms. Louis opened the door just a bit and put her head inside. "Mr. DeSai, your expected guests have arrived."

"Show them in, show them in," he said. His voice dripped with eagerness, and this brought a smile to all four of their faces. Candy and Tim both knew exactly who they were here to see; they had just seen him give an interview on television that very morning.

His four new 'family' members entered the office without a shred of apprehension, and now, for the first time since they entered Cliffside, they began to take notice of their surroundings. The entire aesthetic of Mr. DeSai's private workspace consisted of dim lighting and antiques; everything was either mahogany or cast iron, and everything was very detailed and beautiful.

"Sit, sit!" He stood as he spoke, his arms spread out before him as if to say that all they saw was theirs to enjoy. Each one of them took a seat in a different high-backed black leather chair, and instantly they were comfortable.

They were home.

"Ms. Louis, get them whatever refreshments they desire," he told his assistant as he sat back down. His eyes went from one to another, a broad, satisfied smile on his face. "Nothing is too much to ask. They are family. What would you like to drink? Are you hungry?" He knew the answer would be 'no,' and heads simply shook all around.

Ms. Louis nodded, bowing slightly, and quietly left the room. All remained silent at first. Candy, Tim, Pat, and Abby were busy just taking everything in. DeSai, on the other hand, was taking each of them in.

Finally, he spoke to them. "Do you know why you are here?"

This caught their attention finally, and all eyes turned to him, and they were filled with immediate adoration.

"You called us," Tim replied, without a moment's hesitation.

Cyril nodded, filled with pride. "Yes, I beckoned you. I have beckoned you since you arrived at my cave in Honduras. You are my, shall we say, spiritual children. Do you understand?"

They had no ability to understand anything he was saying intellectually, but all of them seemed to have a full grasp of it anyway, and they did not question this. They were clinging to his every word, and they could not pull their eyes away.

"I have called you to welcome you home. Forever I will care for you now, and nothing you need or desire will ever be withheld. You are my children, my lovers… but we have other—family that needs to be brought home as well," he began.

He stood and began to pace slowly before them, his hands clasped behind his back. He wore a long trench coat, and its tails flapped as if in the wind, but no breeze was blowing in the office.

He continued, "I need you to bring me your brothers and sisters. Now, you will not be able to simply bring them. You will need to prove your love to them first, and once you have taken possession of them fully, you will need to mark them as one of us, as it has been done unto you, do you understand?"

"Yes," they all said in unison. Each of them knew what this meant: they would seek out family, make love to them, and taste them; this would be the most satisfying part of all.

"All our family," he finally said. "You will then need to bring them to me; I need to approve. If there is anyone who will prove detrimental to our lives, it will need to be determined by me and me alone. This is never your judgment to make. I base my decision on the knowledge you do not have."

They continued to simply listen intently and keep their eyes on him, entranced by the sound of his voice and the look in his eye. "If you find them attractive and, well, appetizing, then I trust that. Have your fun and bring them home to me. You do not have to accompany them here yourself, but the mark you leave on them will guide them."

Wide smiles spread across each of their faces. He looked at Tim and then Pat. "You two are free to go. It is important that you all keep family business in the…

family. Go about your daily lives as usual, and do not let your activities interfere. It is imperative that we remain under the radar of those who are not yet ours."

Pat rose first, then Tim, both of them filled with eager longing. They had the rest of this day to begin carrying out the directives the 'Master' had given them before returning to their daily jobs. They didn't want to waste a minute.

"I'll see you both soon. Have fun, boys…" DeSai said, his own smile growing.

When the doors were closed behind them, DeSai turned his full attention to Abby and Candy. "While they will use their masculine wiles to bring my daughters, you two should know you are welcome to bring both daughters and sons to me; whatever suits your fancy. I will have my sons continue on a very straightforward quest, but I trust you both to use your own lusts accordingly, whatever they may be," he said, licking his lips lightly. "Now, I should show you exactly what I mean."

With that, Cyril DeSai raised his arms, beckoning for them to draw near. They did so with eager anticipation, and as he wrapped his arms around them both, they became hidden in the dark folds of his coat. The flames of the candles in his office shot powerfully toward the ceiling, and their ecstatic moans could be heard as he began to ravage them.

R.W.K. Clark

CHAPTER 12

Morning came all too quickly. Abby's alarm went off at her usual waking time, but she struggled to get motivated. When she and Candy left the Master's lair, it had been four in the morning; her alarm blared its six-thirty announcement, and she despised the sound immediately. She did not want to work; she wanted to return to Cliffside and allow the Master to do all the things he had done to her last night. She wanted Candy to be there too. It just wouldn't be the same without her.

But he had been very clear on all of his points: it wouldn't be acceptable to deviate from their regular routines. Besides, they all had a lot of work to do, to bring their brothers and sisters home to the Master, just as he had brought them home.

She showered and dressed in a slow, leisurely manner. The memories of the sexual escapade she had experienced with her friend was a powerful memory. The shower was the perfect opportunity for her to relive it in her mind, and to take it out on her body…

By seven-thirty, she was ready to leave her small apartment and go to the mundane grind she had loved only days ago. The fact that she hadn't heard a word from Pat didn't even enter her mind.

∞

Candy came very close to not going to work at all. Since she had become 'enlightened,' she found it to be very pointless, but her desire to please DeSai was so powerful that she simply went through the motions of obedience, and she did this for a couple of different reasons. One, her lust for him was overbearing; she would certainly obey if only to experience his favors once again. But secondly, the thought of what may take place if she disobeyed instilled a dread in her that she had never before experienced.

She showered and dressed as quickly as she could, as she had lain in her bed long after the alarm had gone off. Reflecting on the sex from the night before kept her treating herself for nearly an hour after she had shut it off. She had to run to get to work on time, and she had to struggle to get in the flow again once she was there, but most of her day would consist of thinking about her Master, and when she might be with him again.

Finding his daughters and sons and marking them would be the fastest way.

∞

Pat Gilliam woke in a strange bed, next to a strange blond woman. She slept soundly, and he stared at her face. She was attractive, and she smelled good; she had tasted even better. Her long hair was fanned out over her pillow, and he could clearly see the mark he had left;

the Master would summon her soon.

He had met her after leaving Cliffside and returning to the city. He had intended to hit a bar several miles from his home to begin hunting; it wouldn't do to go to one of their regular hangouts; this would certainly draw attention to the family. What he intended to do was begin visiting new places where he wasn't known, so he was going to catch the subway and ride to this new spot in his mind, but it had been unnecessary. He met the blond while riding.

He had never been one to monopolize the attention of the ladies; actually, he had always been considered a bit 'nerdy,' and he had been concerned at first if he could turn on enough charm to get down anyone's pants at all. But as soon as they started talking, she seemed to become putty in his hands; it was far too easy.

He rolled over and looked at a clock on the nightstand: 7:00 am. It was time for him to go. He had done his part, and the Master would do the rest, at least as far as this one went. He would pick up where he left off, seeking another after he had put in his time at work.

His girlfriend since high school, Abigail Cayce, was but a distant memory.

∞

Tim Howell had gotten lucky... very lucky indeed. He had gone directly to the gym when he got back into NYC, and within minutes he had three women standing around him as he worked out bench pressing weights. He had started up a casual conversation about the weather and seemingly swept them off their feet. Asking them to his place for a drink was the next sensible step, and getting all three of them naked once they got there came naturally.

Now he was walking to work and thinking about the hours-long sex the four of them had together. All of that licking and sucking and… biting. Mmmm. If this was the 'task' the Master had given all of them, he was completely game. No arguments from him.

Suddenly a face came to mind, a woman's face. He knit his brow as he tried to recall who this person was. Her face was certainly familiar; if he weren't having such a problem bringing her name to mind, he would swear he knew her well. As he thought about her, it suddenly occurred to him.

It was Candy. His girlfriend.

No emotions or feelings of love or adoration filled the void in him when she was in his mind's eye. That quickly he knew their long-term relationship was over. He felt no remorse whatsoever.

He arrived at the place where he worked and grabbed the door handle, pulling it so he could enter. The scent of perfume filled his nostrils, and he turned to see from whom the distraction was coming. It was Jennifer Mills, one of his co-workers.

"Well, hello Jen," he said, his voice husky and his eyes cloudy. "Don't we smell wonderful today?"

The woman looked in his eyes. "Thank you, Tim. Are you okay? Did you get… a haircut… or something?"

He smiled, flashing her his most dashing grin. "No, Beautiful. Why do you ask? Does it really look shorter?"

"No, no. Just something is… different," she replied.

He nodded and held the door wider for her to enter. "Yes, you would be correct; something is different. If you're lucky, I may just get you alone later and tell you all about it…"

∞

Cyril DeSai sat in his office, comfortable in his leather chair. His head was back, and his eyes were closed. He had a very content, almost smug, look on his face; he was smiling.

On his lap sat a large cat with long black fur which was beautifully streaked with silver in all the right places. He stroked it happily, and its purr was nearly deafening. This cat brought his hollow soul such peace.

They were doing everything correctly, and DeSai couldn't be more pleased. At the rate they were going, he was going to turn this town upside down in no time at all. The sheer size of it meant nothing to him; with each and every bite, a new child was born, and with that scores more would be introduced to him. In six months, no one would know what hit them. In a year, there would be no one left to wonder.

Maybe this time, this century, he would discover his missing half, his eternal mate, his mighty minion. This is all he had ever sought, and the special someone had remained forever elusive, leaving him to search, end it all, and begin again for centuries.

But he had a stirring inside of him that he couldn't

quite identify. It yanked and pulled at his black heart and mind, and he was sure he was closer to finding her than ever. He would find his queen here, in this filthy, forsaken place, and he would take her hand, and she would rule beside him until the planet ceased to exist. If he had his way, this would be much sooner than later.

He knew precisely the activities of his four new loves; they had done extremely well. While the girls were getting a late start, they were enthralled with the lust that encompassed being a vampire. All four of them had already forgotten love, both as an emotion and as an action. He filled them now, and as the changes began to snowball in their beings, he would take more and more control until their own persons were no more. If he found a weakness in them at any time, well, there always comes a time when one would be sacrificed for the greater good.

"Isn't that so, Elsa?" He lifted the feline on his lap until he could look into its green eyes. "You will have a mother soon, and I will have a wife. Yes, girl." He kissed the cat on the nose and then let it drop to its feet on the floor. It scooted away and curled up in front of the fireplace, which he kept burning at all times.

He closed his eyes once more. He could hardly wait for the new ones to come tonight. Perhaps, she would be among them. Finally, the searching would be over. Finally, he would be complete.

CHAPTER 13

The waiting was always the most difficult part, and he attributed this to an eternity of life.

For each and every bite, new slaves would come, and this began almost immediately after he sent out those who were first. This proved to be true this time also, and DeSai was filled with an eagerness that perhaps the next woman, or the next after her, would be the one to kindle the flame in his dead heart and become his queen.

After he sent forth the four who had found his cave, the ball began rolling very quickly, and like those before them, the four simply faded a bit into the back of his mind. He still soothed them with comforting lies, and he always made provision for their each and every need, and he would continue to do so. The fact of the matter was that Cyril DeSai was on a mission to make the world his own for eternity and to do that he would need his queen. He would not rest until he found the one who stirred him.

The men who came to him after being bitten were always given their directive and then sent on their way. They were an integral part of his kingdom because they would bring him the most women. Once he enlightened them, they could live by instinct, and he let them, unless they came to him for something, of course.

But the women he always 'sampled' before he sent them out. If after he had them, he knew they were not the one, he would simply send them forth as well into the hunt. Most of them would bring him more men; this was to be expected. Some of them would lure women to him, and this always pleased DeSai to no end. The thought that his new queen may be so… adventurous… always brought a pang of hunger to him that he feared would never be satisfied. His favorite part of being who he was, aside from the ravenous feeding, was the intense sex he had on a daily basis.

So, the four did well in their conquests. The women literally began to pour in, and while most of them were only yawn-worthy, in his opinion, there were those he needed to sample more than once to be sure she was not the one.

The first that grabbed his attention a second time was a raven-haired temptress named Nicole. She had walked alone into his office, which was rare, and she had a light in her eyes that most did not have at this point. She was intelligent and beautiful, with breasts that knew no gravity, and a flavor that nearly made him powerless to stop once he began. On the first night, he used her mercilessly, and she liked it. This compelled him to summon her once again, and their lovemaking had been just as passionate as before.

She had walked into his office smiling. "I knew you

would want me again."

Cyril smiled and quietly approached her. He grabbed her long hair and pulled her head back, planting rough kisses on her neck that drew moans from the pits of her body. He had torn her clothing from her and held nothing back as he threw her down and thrust himself into her again and again. His intended mate would love the violence of it, and this Nicole had great potential, but when they were finished, she began to show a level of possessiveness that was utterly distasteful to him. She also began to be snide regarding the level of force he had used with her. No queen of his would even have enough soul left inside of her to care about either issue.

So she was gone, sent out to do the work of the other slaves.

His species was slowly but surely gaining ground. During the first two months, newly acquired family members came quickly, but sporadically. As his family grew, his senses went into overdrive, and he knew he was gaining ground faster than he could have ever imagined.

There was a second benefit to doing things the way he did them. Not only did his slaves come to him willingly, offering themselves to him and his purpose without hesitation, but they would also begin to take ill if they were not strong enough to conform to their new state of being properly. They would be fine and functional for a while, but after a time their bodies would simply reject his life-altering venom. They would go to work in the day, functioning normally, without anyone around them being at all aware of their state. At night, they would hunt and do his bidding. Inevitably, though, his bite would take hold of any soft spots they may have, whether it be physical, mental, emotional, or otherwise. The condition would worsen until the individual was wiped out altogether.

This ensured the strength of his army, and it did so without requiring him to dirty his hands at all.

The twenty-third woman who came to him at Cliffside was a perfect example. She had come to him with lust-filled eyes and blood-red lips, and the sound of his voice had been enough to lure her directly into his arms. She was a vixen, but even as he ran his tongue over her nipples and drove it between her legs, he knew she possessed a kind of weakness, though he could not identify it specifically. The sex was raunchy, brilliant really, but there was a scent about her that told him something was very wrong. The bite of a minion had the same effect as if he had done the biting himself, so he finished with her and sent her out among the masses.

Two days later, he had sensed her loss, as he did whenever one of his family left the world of the living. He stole into the night and visited the place she lived, where he discovered insulin used to treat diabetes. When he read the obituary in the papers, which had been submitted by her family, it stated she had suffered mass kidney failure, though she had shown no signs of problems and had been young. Yes, diabetes had taken over her now-dead body like wildfire, thanks to the bite. He wouldn't have to worry about weeding her out; her body had done it for him.

Cyril DeSai had adjusted to the familiar routine of spending his days and evenings instructing the new men and sending them out while feasting on the souls of each and every woman who was undergoing the change. Within him, he knew he would find his queen soon; it tugged at his black heart, and he was constantly filled with anticipation.

Any day now.

So, the strong got stronger, and the weak died off fast. If one were to hover in space and view things from afar, they wouldn't be able to see anything amiss. His slaves held down their jobs and maintained their homes, and they plucked people up one by one, to simply bite them and to feed off them. The family rapidly grew.

The way he had his minions handle this issue was to recruit those in positions of power, thus spreading the walking death into the most important places as quickly as possible

It was working wonderfully. Within six months, New York was beginning to look more like home to him than any place had in three-hundred years.

The entire world would be his and do his bidding, just as it should be.

R.W.K. Clark

CHAPTER 14

Cyril DeSai was stepping into the position he had worked for since he became the monster that he was, and the world was none the wiser.

Only three short months after releasing the first four of his slaves, he stepped into a greater position of respect in society. His venom had spread to such an extent at that point that most of the authority figures in the great city had joined his family, and they were all working diligently to make sure nothing interrupted the flow of growth that was taking place.

Two of the first had already died; the first one, Tim, had an existing, yet unknown, heart condition, and his body failed him during the second month. Candy was the second. She had been an alcoholic, and her penchant for drink grew increasingly worse and worse until her body gave out as well. But his family had continued to grow, with only the weak and deranged dregs of society wiping themselves out while the strong and intelligent continued to flourish.

Cyril sat in his darkened office and pondered these facts. Now all of the staff at Cliffside Wineries belonged to him, and if not for his great love of wine, he would have shut the place down right away; no need for its cover any longer, after all. Indeed, the world continued to function beautifully, but many of the smaller details had already begun to fade out of human routine.

He considered the fact that money was being obliterated among his people; there was simply no need for it! When one of them would visit a place that required the normal use of currency they would always oblige, but soon enough that area would be grafted into his poisonous tree as well, and that would cease.

He was spreading. Spreading like a disease, and still, he had yet to find the One.

He began attending city government functions during the third week of the first month, and he topped his initial introductions off by contributing great amounts of cash to the city itself. It was all done under the guise of 'cleaning the place up' and beautification. Things began to rapidly improve on all accounts, and why shouldn't they? Even the vagrants and junkies were his now, and there was no longer a need for them to indulge themselves in the lifestyles they had been living.

Crime rates went down drastically. Bums disappeared from the streets. Everyone was smiling, quiet and peaceful. Everyone was in love; they were in love with him. He controlled everything right down to the finest detail. Only tourists and top government officials on the state and federal levels were none the wiser.

But they would be soon enough.

The search for his queen continued, and he became

even more obsessed with finding her with each passing day that gave him more and more power. Into his third month, and well into his establishment in local government, he again thought he may have found her.

The third woman to catch his powerful fancy went by the name Sophie, and Sophie was a native of Brazil who had bleached her hair platinum blonde. She was no ordinary woman though, not by a long shot, and DeSai quickly became preoccupied with her.

She was in the States studying to become an attorney, and her great hope was to get into politics. She held an internship at the governor's office, where she was very dedicated to her education and future. She was bright, beautiful, and very intriguing.

The governor himself bit this one and brought her to DeSai personally, as pleased with himself as a cat who brings his owner a mouse which is still living. Cyril could see why; she was breathtaking, and even while in a trance his venom and voice held her in, she was able to stand alone with her mind. This was a beautiful thing for him.

"Master DeSai," said Governor Coretti on that day, "This is Sophie. She is an intern at my offices, and very valuable to our local government. The girl has a very bright future indeed. I thought you would want to get to know her as soon as possible." Coretti bowed his head before DeSai, who couldn't take his tar-black eyes from her brown ones.

He nodded in response, then said, "Indeed, I would like that very much, James. Leave us. I know you have other prospects, yes?"

Again the governor bowed, and he backed from Cyril's office without even a reply. He knew that obedience was best; it was what was instilled in all of his children thanks to the loving bite.

When the doors were closed, he spoke to the edible beauty. "Sophie. Welcome. Why don't you show me what you can do, my dear."

A smile crept across her stunning face, and she slowly reached behind her and unzipped her dress. She did this with stunning grace, using her curves as weapons in a slow, tantalizing dance which had DeSai stricken.

She allowed the dress to drop to the floor, and beneath she wore undergarments like those he saw only in ads on billboards. He lowered his gaze to her gorgeous body, and his penis immediately became rock-hard. She was amazing.

Cyril lowered himself into his chair and continued to watch her half-naked body sway to absolutely no music at all, at least none that could be heard. He was sending the music to her.

Could she be the one? His rotting heart was beating very, very fast.

Next, she unclasped her bra and then dangled it from her polished forefinger. He could smell her scent powerfully; she was not defective, at least not that he could tell. She turned around revealing black transparent panties which showcased her rear beautifully; it was the perfect shape of a heart.

He rose. He was becoming very uncomfortable sitting like this.

"I want to taste you," he said to her. His voice was deeper, husky with desire. Her back was still to him, and she responded only by lowering her panties until they fell to the floor.

DeSai crossed his office, loosening his trousers as he went. Oh, how he hoped it was she. He took a seat in one of the black leather recliners near the fire and proceeded to put up the footrest. She slowly approached him, a smile on her face, her eyes clouded over from her own lust.

When she reached him, she put one knee on each armrest, straddling him as he sat in the chair. He could not resist her; her scent was floral, and very, very strong indeed. He raised his hands and placed them on her hips. At first, he was gentle, stroking her body with soft caresses. He sat up slightly and began to stroke her breasts, using his thumbs to tweak her nipples. She threw her head back, and a growl escaped her throat.

Suddenly with great force, he buried his head between her legs, holding her against him at the small of her back. His tongue was rough, he knew this, and usually, he was much more careful with the new slaves, but this one had pushed him over a line. She attempted to pull back, but the animal in him became more determined than ever, and he licked her harder and harder. Now she began to struggle in earnest, and pained cries were escaping her lips.

"Please," she sobbed. "It hurts."

He pushed her away from him violently, his eyes rimmed in red, the irises blacker than ever. She had weakness in her that was unacceptable, even for a mere slave.

"Why do you weep?" His voice was a low sneer, and he had a smile on his face. His erection had immediately disappeared, for nothing destroyed his sexual appetite more than the whining of a full-grown woman.

Her arms flew downward without shame, and she uncovered her breasts for his view. Now he was content. He stood and took two long strides. As soon as he reached her, he grabbed her by her waist and lifted her naked body up off the ground. He looked up at her face as he carried her back to the chair, kneeling her just in front of him.

With a close eye, he continued to watch her as she increased the pressure on his penis in her bare hands. She began to lick slightly and then began to desperately drink at his manhood, to no avail. He was beginning to tire of this cat and mouse game. Why had she not simply let him master her body, as well as her soul?

He gave a quick jerk of his wrist and motioned her to leave. It was always good for him to catch this type of weakness right away so he could send her away with the other slaves. Not to mention the fact that her beauty will bring more to his family.

Cyril DeSai let the beautiful young Brazilian student and intern leave effortlessly to the door in full control.

She had certainly not been the one.

CHAPTER 15

New York City, Two Years Later

It took only two years for him to claim his throne, and the world had indeed become his. The only thing missing was a throne next to his, and a mate to sit in it. This was the only thing that would ever fully satisfy him.

He loved all the sex, and there were times he indulged himself to his heart's content more than fifteen times a day. On the days when he was feeling the emptiness of his own solitude, he had difficulty performing more than four or five times, but because it was a purely physical act for him, and because it was the only thing that truly distracted him, he fed his addiction to the female form as he pleased.

Mostly he would use his women slaves at his whim, and they would cooperate. But when the urge to be rough and cause pain came, he would indulge it fully. At times, especially if they were too new, they would become frightened. While most endured the torture he would bestow on them, there were always those who whimpered. Using his mind control, he could pre-screen them in a flash more quickly and efficiently, before they even came to him; some he would use to satisfy his blood-hunger to a certain point and send them away.

∞

It was a beautiful starlit evening two years to the day after Candy, Abby, Tim, and Pat had sat in Cyril DeSai's office receiving their 'welcome' and instructions from the Master regarding what they were to do with their 'lives' from then on. Now the Master stood in his office tying a long narrow black necktie, without the use of a pesky mirror, of course. He was thinking about that morning, in particular, the morning they walked into his life. That was the beginning of the end of mankind as the world knew it. He had been aware of that, even then. Beginning again in a city this size had been the best decision he had ever made. In the past, he had chosen small towns due to their lack of knowledge and power, but this had been a smashing success.

Tonight, beneath the stars and spotlights, Cyril DeSai, a winemaker from an unknown place, would take his place as ruler in the great American government. Democracy? What democracy? Natural-born-citizen clause? Forgotten.

He was going to be in charge fully. Everything he had ever wanted now belonged to him. His slaves continued to assimilate themselves into each neighboring society, bringing the new ones to him, and spreading like a disease. In another year, the world, in its entirety, would belong to him.

He had chosen his 'date' for the festivities from the droves of new women who had come to him last week. He had his way with her the night of their first introduction, and he was looking forward to it once again. She had been thrilled with the pain he had inflicted on her, and when he got to know her a bit better afterward, he understood why. She had fully enjoyed pain before her change. He would keep her around. Someone like that would always come in handy to him.

Her name was Miranda, and she wore her hair long and straight, blonde with a layer of black underneath. She enjoyed circling her eyes in deep black, and she wore her makeup very light, almost white. Having this one on his arm on this all-important night would be perfect; her appearance complimented his well, although she wasn't altogether his taste.

For the first time in his eternity, he was growing bored with the search for his queen. The surety he had felt over the years that he would find her soon still nagged at him, but the ache inside of him drove him to push that to the back of his mind. Now he simply lived each day using anyone he could get his hands on. The new ones who came were only used; he stopped being eager in regard to learning their likes, dislikes, and personalities. He found each disappointment surprisingly painful, and he was exhausted with the ache.

He tightened the tie and straightened it before donning a long-tailed formal jacket. It may have been a bit out of the current style, but it suited him wonderfully. Funny, but he had taken notice that his minions had abandoned their traditional love of clothing fads, and they had begun dressing in a manner which was much more similar to his own taste. Mind-control and lust were beautiful things indeed.

Lastly, DeSai took a comb to his long black hair and combed all of it back, catching it in the ponytail he wore down his back. He used a bit of hairdressing to hold it in place before placing an elastic on it to tie it down. He looked… ravishing. He laughed aloud.

A light knock on his office door told him his helicopter would be waiting to transport him to Washington, D.C., and Miranda would be waiting on board for him. He loved how she stared at him constantly, as though her eyes could not soak him up fast enough. She was not the one, but she would definitely do for now.

Ten minutes later, he was on the chopper, and they were on their way to the nation's capital, where Cyril DeSai would take power over the country. From there, he would certainly have the entire planet. He could barely contain himself.

They climbed from the chopper to be greeted by screams and great cheers. While most of the hundreds in attendance, as well as the observers, were his own, there were literally thousands, both in person and watching television, who had yet to join the family. They must not be clued in as to the truth. It was always their learning which caused his detriment, each and every time. He had come way too far now. He would not let it happen again. He would be patient, very patient.

Miranda was lovely this night. She wore a silk jersey dress with a belt which knotted to the side. On her somewhat large feet, she wore spiked black satin heels, and her make-up was perfect. Every man who saw her followed her with his eyes, both slaves and the living alike. This did not bother Cyril in the slightest. He would have her this night, just as he would any night he desired. They could have her on the other nights. She meant nothing to him. She was only… meat.

The ceremony which recognized the winemaker also served to 'swear him in.' This entertained him. What was he swearing to, exactly? Ah, yes. He was swearing to run the show for all time. He could hardly wait for all the hubbub to die down, for the cameras to stop their flashing and the interviewers to disappear, but they would be following him for the duration of the night. They need to get their fill of him and put him in their pages and on the TV screens. Patience, President DeSai, your time has not yet come in full.

Now the celebration began, an overwhelming party with thousands of his slaves in attendance, while others roamed the earth to continue the 'good work.' He and Miranda took their seats, his being the seat of honor. It was official now: Cyril DeSai had finally come to a level of power he had only dreamed about.

As he sat and the festivities went on around him, he smiled to himself and thought about when all of this had truly begun. Oh, the struggles he had been through to get to this point. The times he had thought his number was up, but he had made it for hundreds of years now.

1642 France

He let himself remember… France,

"Cyril, one of the men, is outside. He says they need you in the vineyard. Problems with some of our grapes." Cecile, his dear wife, smiled as she stood in the doorway of their home, her long blonde hair flowing out behind her as the wind played with it.

He could not help but smile back; even now he could hear the sound of the children playing outside behind her, and all was perfect in his world. He loved to have his midday meal at home every day. He loved to see the sunlight in his wife's hair. In all of his thirty-six years, he had never seen another as beautiful as his Cecile.

"Do you know what the problem may be?" he asked.

She simply shook her head, the smile still on her glowing face. "No, my darling. It is Marquis, and he simply said that something looks to have gone wrong with an entire row."

DeSai owned a vast vineyard and made the very best wines in all of France. Cyril took great pride in what he produced, and this fact drove him to seek perfection, in all he did. The characteristic had brought him great success, and he was well-loved by the French people. He loved them all in return.

His father had taught him: whatever you do, do it with all your might and heart. Do nothing only part of the way. Cyril had lived by this all his life, and it had paid off in all aspects; not only was he a professional success, but he also had the most beautiful wife and children in the region. He had peace in his soul, and his conscience was clear.

He made his way to the vineyard, still smiling as he pondered. Now his mind turned to the problem in the vineyard. The trouble with an entire row? What is Marquis talking about? He had the healthiest crop he had ever had; he was sure the issue was no more than a misunderstanding on the part of his manager; a simple mistake.

He strode to the area with purpose and found Marquis at the main gate. He was leaning against a side support pole and drinking from a cup.

"Mr. DeSai, I hope your meal satisfied," said the manager. "Did your wife tell you I have taken notice of a problem with one of the rows further up-field?"

He nodded and gripped the man's shoulder in greeting. "Indeed. Yes, my meal was delicious, thank you. Let's walk; you can tell me about it on the way."

The two men headed into the vineyard with Marquis leading the way. As they strolled, with purpose, Marquis chatted about his own wife Marian and related to Cyril how their newborn son was doing. After they had walked for about fifteen minutes, the manager turned left and abruptly stopped.

"Here we are, sir," he said. "As you can see, the grapes in this entire row have been trampled, but only here, nowhere else." They began to stroll up the row, and DeSai observed the extent of the damage.

Not only had they been trampled, with hundreds upon hundreds of bunches lying on the ground smashed, but the vines themselves had been broken and torn, literally demolished in many areas.

They reached the end and turned back around and stopped. Cyril stood in silence thinking hard on the confusing dilemma. "What could have done this? It had to have happened during the night, but none of the dogs barked at any time."

"That's strange sir, but since you say it, I have not seen the dogs today at all since I arrived." Now DeSai looked at his employee, and he realized that he had not seen any of the dogs either.

After giving things another look and walking the length of the row once more, DeSai spoke. "I want you to take three men and go look for the dogs, then. I will walk to the manor and see about the ones who stay at the house to alert me. How did I not take notice of these things?"

"I will do it right away sir," replied Marquis, and he began walking towards the vineyard entrance.

DeSai turned back to the row and studied the damage once again. What could have possibly done such harm? It would have taken a single man all night, and he would still not have successfully been able to destroy so many vines. DeSai was at a loss.

Finally, he too strode to the front of the vineyard. He was now sharply aware that he heard no dogs. Their barking was typically ongoing all the time, and the ones who patrolled the vineyard would alert those nearer to the house of any danger. Something was wrong.

By the time he reached the main gate, he was told that Marquis had left according to his directive with three other workers, so he made his way to the main house. He was sure he would find all of the dogs playing to the rear of the manor, or perhaps one had gotten ahold of a wild animal, and they were all feasting. There was an explanation for their absence, he was sure.

His wife came into view, and as he neared, he spoke to her. "Cecile, where are the dogs?"

A look of confusion crossed her face. "The dogs? Why, they are likely out in the field, darling. You just came from there, didn't you see them?"

"They are not there. What about our manor dogs?"

Now she looked concerned. "I have not seen one…" Her voice drifted off as she tried to remember.

The men cared for the dogs by feeding and herding them as needed. Not one of his men had said a word to him about any missing animals. He felt more confused than ever.

"I have sent Marquis and a few other men to find them. They have likely runoff, but an entire row in the vineyard has been completely destroyed, with no logical explanation," he said. "Had the dogs done the damage, it would have been more than a single row." He was speaking more to himself now than to Cecile.

She replied, "I will search around the manor, dear. You tend to your duties."

DeSai nodded curtly and headed back to the vineyard. He chose a couple of good men, and the three of them made their way to the damaged row to begin to clean things up. He pushed the concern for the row itself out of his mind. He was a prosperous vintner, and a single row would not break him.

He was concerned about his dogs.

He and his men worked steadily for three hours cleaning up the mess that had been made in the vineyard before Marquis and the other men returned. "Mr. DeSai!"

Cyril turned his attention to the sound of his name, and he saw his manager approaching from about ten rows down. He began to walk towards him, eager to hear what he and the others had found if anything.

"Give me the news, Marquis!" he hollered as he walked. "Did you find those worthless beasts?" He was smiling, but his smile quickly faded as he took notice of the somber look on the manager's face. When he reached him, Marquis finally spoke.

"Sir, the dogs are on the other side of your property line to the north," he said.

Now DeSai felt confused once again. "Did you bring them back? I will have to punish them to the fullest…"

"No, sir. We did not bring them back." Marquis seemed to be struggling to communicate his thoughts.

Now he was getting frustrated with his manager. "Why did you not gather them and bring them back? We need them here now, as you know full well. I shan't have this damage done a second night."

"Sir, the dogs have all been killed."

DeSai stared at the man incredulously. "Killed?"

"We found them directly on the other side of the property line. They have all been ripped limb from limb; they are barely recognizable. They were in a pile, one atop the others. It makes no sense…" The man's voice trailed off, and he looked utterly frightened.

Now DeSai was getting angry, and he seemed to be in a bit of shock. "Marquis, I have a total of twenty dogs which I use to guard the vineyard and the manor and to alert me as too strange goings-on. What are you talking about?" Surely the man was either mistaken or outright lying.

"Mr. DeSai, sir, I just don't know."

The anger showed on his face now. "Take me," he growled, and the manager turned on his heel, DeSai with him, and they made their way to the wagon which would take them to the place where the dogs supposedly were found.

As they rode, DeSai considered the situation. If they found dead animals, surely it was some other species. Torn limb from limb? Surely his dogs would have put up a havoc of noise at such an assault! Something was wrong.

They arrived on the property's north border and alit from the wagon. Marquis led him along the fence line, and they came to a place where a long branch had been placed in the ground to mark the spot. Marquis himself had placed it there. He stopped in his tracks, turned to his master, and then backed away from the fence warily; he said nothing.

Cyril tore his gaze from his manager's face and stepped up to the fence. He looked over and sucked in his breath sharply. Then he doubled over and lost all that was in his stomach onto the ground.

There, on the other side of the fence, were the bloodied bodies of dogs. They were so badly mutilated they could not be counted. Blood and tissue were puddled and piled here and there, and they were barely recognizable.

But they were his dogs indeed.

He stopped his vomiting and wiped his mouth on the back of his sleeve. When he stood, Marquis was next to him with a metal cup of water from the wagon. He took it gratefully and rinsed his mouth, spitting the water back on the ground. He was afraid to drink any; he would not be able to hold it down, he knew.

"What has happened here, Marquis?" He looked at his manager, but his face was blank. Only his eyes showed his emotions; they were filled with tears.

Never in his years had he seen such a gruesome and unexplainable thing. His stomach sank, and goosebumps broke out all over him. Something was very wrong here.

After a moment, he turned to Marquis. "Gather some gear. Tonight you and I will patrol the vineyard while it is dark. We will see if the culprit returns, and if he, or it, does, they will pay for this with their very life."

"Yes, sir," Marquis replied, and the men returned to the wagon and made their way back to the vineyard, discussing the situation with great disgust and anger the entire way.

∞

"Are you okay, Master?" It was Miranda speaking to him. DeSai came out of his reverie and looked at her.

He replied, "Indeed. I am simply enjoying the occasion and the happiness it is bringing. I cannot wait for the entire world to join in our cheer."

"The day will come," she said. She patted him on the leg, running her sharp nails down the length of his thigh, then she turned her attention to a lady friend who was seated next to her. DeSai could have cared less; his mind was a prisoner to the past right then.

∞

DeSai returned to the manor before dark, leaving the rest of the extensive mess for his charges to clean up and rectify. He planned to get a bit of rest before venturing out with Marquis; he would need it.

"Did you find those naughty dogs?" Cecile looked cheerful, but her eyes were apprehensive. He knew she had looked and found nothing; she had to be concerned.

He nodded slowly. "Yes, but it is not good, my darling."

"What is it, Cyril?"

He sat his wife down and then directed the children to prepare for bed. They immediatly obeyed, and after they were out of earshot, he sat across the table from Cecile and took her by the hand.

"The dogs were found on the north side of the

property. All have been killed," he began, cautiously.

Her eyes grew wide. "Killed? What do you mean, 'killed'?"

DeSai chose his words wisely; he did not fancy frightening his wife. He told her they were all found together, and he credited the deed to bandits who may want to rob the property. He then told her the plan he and Marquis intended to execute that very night.

Cecile was not happy with the revelation of their scheme, but she did not argue. She kissed and embraced him with tears in her eyes. She worried for him, and he did not blame the girl, but he would not allow some criminals to take all they have, to threaten their happiness and livelihood any more than they already had.

Cyril made his way to their chambers and lay down on the bed, but he would get no sleep. He tossed and turned, the vision of the ravaged dogs very clear in his head. It had been a scene worse than any nightmare he had ever had.

He rose when the moon was clear in the sky, and he dressed warmly, making sure to load his weapon and pack a small bag with other small items they may need: a knife and extra ammunition. He felt excitement at the thought of doing to the culprits what they had done to his dogs, and possibly what they wanted to do to him and his family.

He would have none of it.

Marquis was waiting outside for him in the wagon. He had brought along coffee for drinking, to help them stay alert during their patrols. He intended to do this every night until the savages were caught and punished; coffee would be needed.

They began at the vineyards. They left the wagon at the gate, as the vineyard area was only suited for walking, and they began to patrol the rows. It would be a daunting task; the vineyard was a massive place. They walked in silence, each man walking the row next to the other. They would not go out of earshot of each other in case one or the other encountered trouble.

They kept their ears open, and their lanterns lit, but the vineyard proved clean; not even the sound of a breaking branch was heard during their search. It was time to take the wagon and patrol the rest of the land, beginning with the grounds around the manor, then they would patrol the perimeter. If all this turned up nothing, they would begin the process again, and they would do this until they found the answers they were looking for. Cyril DeSai was a determined man.

As the wagon approached the manor, both men quietly discussed where they should begin. As they passed the front of the house, Marquis suddenly grabbed DeSai's arm violently, and in response, DeSai brought the wagon to an abrupt halt.

"Sir, the manor door is ajar…"

DeSai's head jerked in response toward the front of the house. Yes, the door of the manor was indeed wide open. Dread filled his stomach as he tried to remember whether or not he had secured it; he was certain he had. The safety of his wife and children was paramount to him. He would not have neglected that one thing, not to mention the fact that he had a clear memory of doing so.

He looked at Marquis and brought a single finger to his lips, beckoning that they be still. Both men got off the wagon and took their weapons. They slowly and silently crept toward the front of the house, listening. There was no sound, either inside or out.

He leaned toward his manager and whispered, "I will go inside and have a look. You walk around the house and the main grounds, yes?" Marquis nodded and ventured into the darkness with his lantern.

DeSai crossed the door's threshold and entered his home. Initially, he stood on the rug in the foyer and held the light out in front of him. Nothing at all looked out of place; everything was as it should be. He stealthily made his way to the dining and kitchen areas, but all was as it should be. Now he would look in on Cecile and the children.

He crept up the massive staircase which led to the sleeping quarters. The room which he and Cecile occupied was the master bedroom directly to the right at the top of the stairs; he would look in on her first.

He turned the knob, being very careful to keep quiet; he did not want to wake his wife and put her in a panic. He then held his lantern a small bit into the room, allowing just enough of the light in to get a view of their bed.

It was empty.

Now he flung the door all the way open. "Cecile?

Cecile!" There was no response, only the wind blowing through the open window.

He frantically made his way around the room, but she was not there. She must be in with the children, as she probably didn't want them to sleep alone that night. He sighed and made his way out of the room and down the hall to the next doorway, which was the room where both his son and daughter slept.

This door was wide open, and his heart skipped a beat. This should not be.

He entered, allowing the full light of the lantern to illuminate the interior. Within seconds he saw them. All three of them.

They lay on the floor atop the main rug which was the centerpiece of the room. Both children's bodies had no head; their heads lay next to each of them respectively. Blood was everywhere.

It was then he realized that the figure between the two children was his beloved Cecile. Her throat had been cut so deeply that her head lay in a horrible, unnatural position. Her eyes were wide open, and a look of terror was spread over her face. She had died feeling petrifying fright and grief; it was all over her face.

For the second time that day, Cyril DeSai was sick. He vomited until there was no more to vomit, and then his stomach continued to heave painfully for a long time after. When he was finished, he struggled to clear his thoughts and get his wits about him. What to do?

Finally, a shred of clarity came: he had to get to Marquis! Something very, very bad was here…

He took his lantern and his firearm and ran out the bedroom door, and now he was not concerned about being still; there was simply no one left to wake.

"Marquis!" His footsteps pounded down the staircase, and he ran to the foyer and out the door. "Marquis!"

His manager shouted back, "Sir!" and DeSai began to run to the sound of his voice, lantern bobbling back and forth before him, its light bouncing to and fro erratically.

He saw his charge's lantern, and in seconds, could clearly see the form of the man standing before him. He slowed to catch his breath and began to speak.

"Marquis, they have been murdered! All three!" He doubled over in an effort to catch his breath. "My family is dead!"

The manager began to respond as DeSai tried to breathe. "Dead, sir? What are you…?" Marquis' voice went silent.

Cyril's head jerked up. Marquis' lantern lay on the ground, it's light flickering dangerously. The manager was nowhere.

"Marquis?" He straightened himself out and tried to steady his breathing. He held his own lantern out and turned in a complete circle. "Marquis!"

Suddenly, he heard the rushing of the wind around him, and it was accompanied by a sound very much like clean clothing blowing in the wind as it dried. He turned in circles quickly, trying to see anything, but there was nothing to see.

Then behind him, something hit the ground hard. He turned and lit the area up with his light. It was all he could do to keep himself from screaming.

Marquis lay in a pile not five feet from him. Blood was pouring from a gaping wound on his neck. His eyes were open, and he was looking at his master for help. His mouth was moving, trying to form words, but no sound came out of his lips.

"Marquis!" He rushed over to his manager, and he could immediately see that Marquis would die within seconds. Suddenly, the man's mouth stopped moving, and his eyes went like glass; he was gone that fast.

DeSai's mind began to swim, and he was overcome with vertigo. He dropped to his knees, the lantern hitting the ground beside him; it remained upright and lit. He placed both of his fists in the dirt before him to keep himself from completely fainting, and he forced his breaths to come more slowly. He must get his wits about him, he had to figure out what was happening. Was he dreaming, or was all of this real?

He looked up at Marquis lifeless body before him; indeed, this was very real. Now he sat back on his own haunches and opened his ears; whoever had just done this thing to his manager, whoever had killed his family and his dogs, was still here.

That was all it took. He stood to his feet, grabbing up his lantern as he went. Suddenly he felt much calmer. He would kill this thing and dispose of it properly before it took his life and the lives of his other charges as well.

"Cyril, Cyril, why do you believe you have an understanding which you do not have?"

The voice was very low, and it was very, very close. He jumped in his own skin and once again began to turn round and round, illuminating all he could with the powerless lantern.

"Who is it? Who are you?" He yelled this loudly, even though he knew they could hear him clearly. He wanted to instill fear in the person with the sound of his voice, but he could hear how badly it really shook. He was the one who was afraid.

"It is I, your new master…" Suddenly he was enveloped in an embrace from behind. He tried to turn his head to see who had hold of him, but just as he craned his neck he felt the sting there; he was being bitten by… something.

DeSai screamed loudly, and he tried to struggle against the arms which held him, but to no avail. Then, as quickly as they had grabbed him, the arms disappeared.

Now he fell to the ground entirely. He was cold, so cold. He trembled and shook, and a sound like roaring waves filled his ears. His entire body was wracked with pain, and then all of a sudden all was still once more.

"You will continue where I am forced to leave off," the voice told him. His eyes were open, and he looked around as best he could without moving his head; he could not move it at all. But no one was within his line of vision; nothing and no one.

The words continued. "Finally, my years draw to an

end, but I lived to continue the life with you. Now I will gladly lie down in surrender; the stake in my chest causes me an overwhelming pain. Carry on for me, Cyril. You are the ideal choice…"

The sound of flapping surrounded him, and suddenly the wind died. All was still once again. He lay on the ground shaking violently, and his vision had tinges of red around it. What had happened?

∞

Now DeSai snapped out of his haze and took notice of the inaugural festivities which were going on around him. He smiled with black joy; all of this was exactly what the voice had been talking about. It was what he had been striving for all these centuries, and he was accomplishing the mission. Soon, the whole world would be a part of his kingdom; it would all be his.

"President DeSai, it is time to give interviews to the press," said a young man in a red tie, Martin Lamb. He had been assigned to handle the inevitable publicity which would result from the gaining of his new position. "This will be done here, but we will step inside to avoid all the chaos, sir. The members of the press are all inside and waiting for you."

He looked up at the man and smiled, then stood. "Yes, Mr. Lamb. I'm ready." He turned to Miranda. "I will return shortly. Enjoy a good time, my darling." He then followed the man out of the room.

He knew that the majority of journalists and reporters would belong to him already, but there would be those who were still members of the soon-extinct 'normal' society. It was for the benefit of these that the world continued to keep up appearances; not until the very last was enslaved would they all begin to live the way decent vampires should.

He walked up to the small stage and the microphone laden podium with the Presidential Seal on it. A hush fell over the room, and he took his place before all of the reporters who had packed in for this moment. He was on a cloud; he had arrived. It had been a very long road.

∞

After being bitten by the unseen stranger, Cyril was not the same. He spent the remainder of that night pacing the vineyard and manor grounds. He visited the bodies of his wife and children, but things had changed in his body at a lightning pace. He ended up feasting on what fresh blood he could draw from them. He had been appalled at this, even as he did it, but he felt powerlessly driven, and he followed through.

Afterward, he felt much stronger, and he proceeded out to where the body of Marquis was lying lifeless on the ground. He drained him, and once he was finished, he stood and looked around. It was funny how clearly he could see in the darkness.

He was a monster now, and he knew it with a certainty which he didn't understand. He would come to understand it, but for now, he simply accepted it. He would simply… survive, and that is what he did.

He listened to his gut and the compulsions which now controlled him. In time he came to understand it:

he was a vampire. He needed others like him, and it was up to him to create them. He needed a queen, but no other like Cecile would be found. This compulsion was something he pushed aside daily until he could push it aside no more. It was the resulting acts, spurned by these two instincts, which caused him to settle here and there, making slaves and taking lives. It was these that caused him to run when the hunting always began, and it was an instinct which had led him to his inner sanctum, the cave in the depths. The one before him had lived here as well, he knew this with certainty. Now the cave was his.

He would live forever, his body an empty black shell, but he would not do it alone. Over and over he would begin, and over and over he would fail.

But not this time.

∞

DeSai took notice of all the faces looking at him expectantly as he stood at the podium before them. He opened the conference by offering a speech which consisted of so many lies: how honored he was to accept the responsibilities given him; how proud he was to be able to serve the public. It poured like liquid silk from his lying lips.

He then welcomed questions, and just as he suspected, one of his very own began.

"President DeSai, when will you be relocating from Cliffside to take up residence here at the White House?"

He smiled his most impressive grin at the man, who was simply glowing at the fact that his Master stood at the podium before him. "I will be fully moved in by tomorrow, and am greatly looking forward to the change. Thank you."

A woman stood next, another of his own. "Who will take over your Cliffside Winery responsibilities, sir?"

"I have chosen businessman Martin Steenway of Atomic Technologies. He is a brilliant businessman who has personal experience with winemaking; I have tasted his private products, and they impressed me to the point that I knew he was the best choice for the job," said Cyril. "I am also confident that he will do things at Cliffside the way I would want them done."

Now a woman in the rear of the crowd stood from her chair. She was not one of his, but she was quite beautiful; she certainly would be.

"Yes, dear. You in the back," he said to her.

"President, are you also confident that your experience running a winery qualifies you to run a country?"

DeSai kept his dazzling smile plastered to his face. "What is your name, my dear?" Her slight accent told him she was not American, at least not by birth.

"Rasia Engres. I am with the Kiev 'Post'. I hail from Ukraine, sir," she replied all business.

She was simply striking. She had red hair, fiery red, and it was pulled back out of her face in a simple, yet formal, style. Her makeup was flawless, and the colorations of it set off her deep green eyes beautifully. She had the eyes of a cat.

DeSai blinked twice. "I am not only confident in my

own abilities, Miss Engres, but I have full faith in the knowledge and abilities of my many advisors. This will be a team effort," he lied.

The woman jotted something in a small notebook and then took her seat. He had not been able to tantalize her; was she simply too far from him? Her entire demeanor reflected a lack of interest in DeSai for anything other than business; this intrigued and thrilled him through and through.

"Mr. President…!" The voices all took off at once now, and flashes from cameras began to go haywire. He turned his attention to the task at hand, answering questions and keeping up appearances.

But Rasia Engres kept a firm grip on his mind.

R.W.K. Clark

CHAPTER 16

"Tell me, Mr. Lamb, who was the reporter seated near the back? The woman with the red hair?" DeSai and Lamb were on their way back to the party after the press conference.

Lamb slowed his pace. "She is not yet with us, sir."

"But who is she?"

"She is a reporter who often frequents American government events such as this one. She is well known to others in the White House," he replied. "If you would like more information I will check with your public relations team. I am fairly new to this, as you know. I mostly know of her from the television press conferences of the past. She has been around for a couple of years. That's all I know."

While DeSai couldn't let thoughts of this woman take over on this night, he did indeed keep her in the front of his mind. He spent the rest of the evening going through the motions: dancing with Miranda and others, clinking glasses with the men, and showing off his finely-tuned personality at the right times.

But how had she dodged the bullet of his control thus far? The question plagued his thoughts all evening.

He and Miranda stayed at the White House that night, and when they took to their room, he was still obsessing to himself over the strange woman.

"You are distracted, lover," said Miranda once their door was closed and tightly secured. "Would you like to talk it out, or would you prefer to 'work' it out."

DeSai snapped to attention, and he looked over at the woman seated on the bed. She wore only a bra and panties, and she was freshening her skin with a touch of perfume. He thought again of the reporter; in the looks department, this woman didn't hold a candle to her. He would be satisfied to use her body, however.

He stood and removed his jacket, and then set his attention on unknotting his tie. He kept his eyes on Miranda, who had a sex-filled smile on her face. "You know, darling that I prefer to 'work' everything out. I have never been much of a talker."

He came and stood before her, bare-chested. She began to kiss his muscled stomach, her eyes closed and her face filled with lust and passion. He watched her go to work on him, unbuttoning his trousers and pulling them down to his feet, along with his boxers. Soon she had him in her mouth, and it felt like magic.

But hers was not the head he wanted to see bobbing up and down on him. He closed his eyes and imagined the head to be that of a distant red-headed reporter. Suddenly his erection grew rock-hard, and Miranda moaned at his physical response.

Cyril allowed the slave to continue pleasuring him with her tongue and mouth, but the scent she commonly wore filled his nostrils. Before, he had found this alluring; now it was nothing more than an annoyance. It interfered with the picture he had in his head of the red-head from the press conference. It was not her scent.

Indeed, he had not been close enough to her to pick up much of anything, and his senses were in a jumble because of all the other people who had been in the room, but this smell was exclusive to Miranda in his mind. He turned to the right and dimmed the lamp on the nightstand; maybe that would help a bit, but he doubted it. He could still clearly see Miranda's two-toned hair in the dark.

Finally, he gave up and decided to keep his eyes closed tightly. He tangled her hair in his fingers and forced her head down on him, then he yanked it back. She didn't gag, but she did moan louder. With his left, he reached down and grabbed her breast, squeezing it roughly through her bra. This turned her on even more.

She pulled away from him and shed the rest of her underclothes from her body. She then lay back on the bed, her elbows supporting her weight. She spread her legs wide, her black pubic hair only a shadow in the dim light. He opened his eyes to gaze at her, but he kept his eyes off her face. He didn't want to be with Miranda, so in his mind, he was not.

He touched her between her legs, softly at first. She continued to look at his face, but he kept his eyes firmly on what he was doing. In his mind, this was Rasia, and he wanted it to stay that way.

"Look at me, Master," said Miranda. The sound of her voice infuriated him, and angrily he thrust his fingers inside of her.

"Do not speak!" His voice growled. She instantly became still, a small whimper the last noise she willing made. He continued with his hand until he was overwhelmed with an angry lust he could not contain. He lowered himself to the floor and knelt before her, then he proceeded to grasp her thighs and yank her body toward him. He buried his face between her legs and feasted on her as she writhed and moaned in pained pleasure, her hands on his head pulling him to her.

This went on for over an hour until she had climaxed too many times to count. He was tiring of this and mounted her. With a sharp thrust, he was inside of her, his hands on her hips, driving himself deeper and deeper into her. He then pulled out and flipped her over, lifting her rear into the air, and he entered her again, with an insurmountable force.

She nearly cried out but bit down on the blanket, which was bunched up in her fists. She enjoyed a bit of pain, and he liked that, but he was genuinely hurting her flesh. If he knew this, it would be the end of her. She let him have his way, and finally, he came and collapsed beside her on the bed.

Miranda lay still next to him, her eyes glued to the digital clock on the nightstand. It was four in the morning. She shifted her gaze to the window, and she saw that the sun was just starting to turn the sky a rich, deep blue. The morning was coming.

"Master…" Miranda spoke softly. He did not respond; he was sleeping now. She rose and walked a pained walk into the bathroom, where she gently closed the door and turned on the light. She looked down and saw her own blood dripping down her legs.

It was time for her to go and work with the others to bring the new ones home. She would not endure this again. She quietly cleaned up and packed her things in the darkness. Within the hour, she was in a cab headed to a hotel near the airport. She knew her new instincts would guide her; she would be fine as one of the slaves.

∞

Cyril DeSai sat having a late breakfast of fruit, bacon, and pancakes on the terrace outside his room. The sun was bright, but he had adapted to that long ago. Contrary to popular fiction, vampires could endure sunlight, they just had to train themselves to take it properly. It barely bothered him at all.

There was a knock on the door of his room.

"Enter," he responded with authority. The door opened, and Martin Lamb stood there, suited up and ready for business.

"Good morning, sir. I hope your night brought you the rest you desired," he began.

DeSai smiled and nodded. "Come in, come in. Have a bite with me."

Lamb closed the door and crossed the room to the sliding doors leading to the patio. He took a seat at the table with the newly sworn-in United States President and began placing various pieces of fruit on the plate before him. He then busied himself with pouring a cup of coffee and adding cream and sugar.

DeSai considered asking the assistant if he knew where Miranda went off to, but in a fraction of a second he decided against it; it didn't matter. She wasn't here. She had served her purpose, and now it was time for her to join the ranks. This was a truth her own new instinct would not let her ignore, and so he knew that was precisely what she had done.

So, on to the next one. The way the strange reporter made him feel, the way she preoccupied his mind, led him to conclude that pursuing anyone else seriously, at least at the current time, would be a waste. He had to satisfy his curiosity, and he was determined to possess, the woman Rasia Engres.

If nothing else, she indeed would become one of the family, at the very least.

As if on cue Lamb said, "I did some checking on Rasia Engres, Master."

DeSai looked up from his plate immediately. "Yes, and what did you discover?"

Martin cleared his throat. "She is indeed from Ukraine. She has been a journalist for six years and has a reputation as being very politically-minded and methodical in her work. My source tells me she is honest and lives according to a very strict code of integrity. I am assuming this is why she has yet to become… one of the family, sir."

Cyril turned this over in his mind without responding. She would not be alone with a man is what he heard Martin saying. This must be how she had slipped through their fingers. He knew this is what Lamb meant when he referred tastefully to her 'integrity.'

"Is she a virgin? This is what you mean, is it not?" He could not keep the eagerness and hope from his voice.

Lamb shrugged. "According to my sources, she has never been known to have a serious or 'long-term' relationship, much less casually date. She is very career-minded, sir. Very focused." He paused and wiped his mouth on his napkin. "As you well know, it would be impossible to determine whether or not she is a virgin without asking her directly, but I can say that she has a reputation for being a bit… frigid."

DeSai soaked up the information like a sponge. "Lamb, I want you to find out more. I want the details. I am considering giving her a personal interview, but I want to know her… intimately first."

"Yes, sir, but how will I find out the personal details? I mean, no one would know these things but Miss Engres herself."

Cyril began to get annoyed with this slave. "Keep it simple, Martin. Did she have a boyfriend in high-school? Was she ever pregnant? Where are her parents? If they were part of our family, I would know it, would I not? Do what I am asking you to do and get back to me as soon as possible." He turned his attention back to his food, dismissing the man with the change of attitude he displayed.

Martin pushed his plate away from him gently and stood; the Master was clearly dismissing him. "Is there anything else, sir?"

DeSai looked up at him and thought for a moment. "Yes. Get me her contact information for myself. If she insists on being evasive about an interview, I may approach things from another angle so it will be necessary. For now, just follow the instructions I have given you."

Martin Lamb bowed slightly at DeSai, then left the Master's room quickly and retreated to his office. He closed the door and secured it behind him before picking up his phone and dialing one of the best investigators in the Washington area, a man who was also one of DeSai's minions.

"Steadman, the Master would like to find out everything he can about the journalist Rasia Engres, the red-haired lady who was in attendance at the press conference last night. He wants to know... everything." Lamb abruptly hung up the phone. Steadman was good; he would be in touch before DeSai knew it.

CHAPTER 17

DeSai's move into the White House went very smoothly. In only a day, everything was complete. While he maintained the façade of a 'president' by keeping his meetings and saving face with other routine activities, his main focus was on the real agenda: bringing more children home to him, for his eternal use.

Those who were weak continued to weed themselves out. One month after he stepped into office, the former President died of a massive brain tumor. Cyril had known it had been there; he could smell its rot clearly. These people were all so vulnerable during the beginning stages. They would either make it or break it. They would thrive, or their own pre-existing weaknesses would eliminate them.

Things were ticking along just like clockwork, and he was thrilled.

New women were brought to him daily by their own new instincts, and he would use them like so much tissue paper. Not one could keep his attention longer than it took to bed them. He would quickly send them out of his presence to join the ranks, and he would spend his alone time thinking about Rasia.

What a beautiful name: 'Rasia.' He had never heard a name that had such a flow and melody. She was a song to him, and just as impossible to grasp.

∞

Lamb had returned to him with more information the very day after their breakfast chat on the patio. DeSai had been filled with hope at what he had learned, but it also served to inform him that he would need to exercise the utmost patience.

"She was raised by a single mother who passed away a year and one-half ago, sir. Ms. Engres was already employed by the 'Post' in Kiev at that time, and she was too busy with her job to even attend her mother's funeral." Lamb's face was stony as he related what he had learned.

This small bit of information pleased DeSai. She was a cold one, his Rasia. This would explain the reason she was a virgin. She had no time for men.

"No boyfriends then, past or present?"

Lamb shook his head. "She has dated briefly in the past. My source was able to contact one of the men, of whom are family to us, Master. His name is Demyan Orlov; he said, in a nutshell, that she would not allow him to touch her, not in a sexual manner anyway. He expressed that she used him to advance, at the 'Post.' He even said some lost their jobs on account of her, and she took their position. This young man is even the nephew of the editor of the Kiev Post, so who knows how she managed to accomplish that feat. It sounds like she has… ice water… running through her veins."

This caused Cyril to smile broadly. This was his dream woman, a girl after his own black heart. Oh, yes, he must know her.

"Contact her and ask her if she would like an exclusive interview with me," he said. He was still smiling, but his eyes were distracted, and his voice was demanding. "I will be flying to Boston today, and I will return tomorrow. Have answers when I return."

Lamb was obviously being dismissed. He rose and left, intent on his mission. It would be to his detriment to not have the requested information on time.

DeSai had gone to Boston for a public appearance and to meet with some city politicians there, all of whom were already in his possession. He answered the questions asked of him by the press, but his mind was on Rasia. She was all he could think about. By the time he was ready to board the helicopter the next morning to return to Washington, he was very lovesick and distracted indeed. He could hardly wait to speak to Martin Lamb.

∞

Cyril DeSai sat at his desk at the Oval Office, the blinds drawn and the lights dim. He wanted his phone to ring, or for Lamb to knock and enter with more information about the elusive Rasia Engres, but all remained still.

This country, yes, and his family all over could pretty much run itself. He took the Presidency for appearances, for the sake of those who were not yet drawn. Otherwise, he was the ruler, but his slaves were no more than animals now, and animals lived by instinct, without rulers. He could take all the time alone he needed.

His taste for the new women had mysteriously dwindled. He had lost much-needed rest turning this over in his mind. In the centuries since he had been turned, he had never experienced such a lack of interest in the raw sex which had come to be his main addiction, next to blood, that is. The new ones would come, and he would throw them an obligatory screwing, but this was mostly because it was expected; it was part of the process.

There was a bite, a special bite, which he had never given to another. It was the one that would make the woman of his choosing his queen for all eternity. It would change her instantly and give her all the strength and power she would need to take her place and rule with him. If the one of his choosing had a weakness, this bite would immediately destroy her; it would take only seconds. This was by design, he knew, even though no one had ever told him that. It was to help him move on and begin looking again right away. But if she were ideal, she would be the strongest and most powerful female on the face of the Earth and all within only moments.

He wanted to bite Rasia. He had seen her only one time, and yet he could not stop himself from thinking about her constantly, day and night. He growled and shook his head as if to empty it of its thoughts, but it did no good, and he began to pace around the office.

Where the heck was Lamb?

Suddenly a sharp rap sounded at the doors, and before it even stopped he responded with an eager, "enter!"

A flustered Martin Lamb appeared and closed the door behind him. "Master," he said, smiling. "I hope your trip went well."

"Yes, yes, as well as can be expected. How are you, Martin? Did you complete your mission regarding Ms. Engres successfully? Have a seat and let's talk."

Both men sat at the desk, and Lamb seemed to be a bit jumpy, but it appeared to be a good thing. He was not nervous; he was a bit excited. DeSai, on the other hand, was more than ready to hear what he had to say.

"You have spoken with Ms. Engres, I take it," he began.

Lamb nodded. "Yes, I have. I related the message to her that you wished to grant her an exclusive interview. She asked why you opted for her, and I told her you wanted the people of Ukraine to get a clear picture of who you are as a man and as a leader, and that you trusted her to provide them with exactly that, based on her professional reputation."

"That's very good, Martin. Very good. What did she say?"

"She is willing to interview you, but she had a couple of… requirements," hc replied.

DeSai began to get confused. "What sort of 'requirements'?"

Lamb took a deep breath; he was treading lightly,

DeSai could tell. "Primarily, she will not interview with you alone."

"What do you mean? That's nonsense!" He began to get a bit hot under the collar. Why did she not want to be alone with him? Was he not attractive enough for her?

His response made Martin flinch slightly, as if he had expected it but still was not prepared for it. "Yes," he began. "She claims she does not interview alone with the opposite sex, and she does not make exceptions to this rule."

At this revelation DeSai was silent. Oh, she was a shrewd one! She maintained control at all times. What was her vision for her final outcome? What was her mind really like? The thought made his crotch tingle erotically.

"What did she propose then?"

Lamb was relieved at his calm question and sighed. "Her photographer is male, a young man who could easily be brought into the family. He acts as her chaperone, so to speak. She will interview you with him present. If not, she would rather wait to speak to you until your next press conference."

Cyril thought only for a moment before saying, "Fine. No problem there. But you think we could bring him into the fold easily. Why is that?"

"He has worked with Ms. Engres since the beginning of his short career, and the boy has absolutely no social life, according to our man Steadman. If we turn him over to one of our beauties, he will not stand a chance."

DeSai did not hesitate. "Arrange it," he said. "and let me know as soon as you find out when she wants to do it."

He dismissed the young man with a curt nod and a glance toward the office door. Lamb jumped up and saw himself out. Now Cyril could go back to his thoughts.

She was the one, he was sure of it. A woman so beautiful, focused, cold, and hard she was meant for him and him alone. She was hungry for advancement, and she wanted to maintain control, not to mention that she was distant and utterly elusive.

But how disappointing it would be if she were not! He could not afford to entertain the thought, and he quickly pushed it out of his head. This was it, he just knew it. He needed to tread very lightly if he wanted to play this one properly; after all, he would be playing for keeps.

Never had a woman had him in such knots! She was completely hard to his advances, and she would not even put herself in a position which would allow him to put his spell on her in order to convince her. Unless she had a normal bite, she would be wary; that was where the control was. He would have to move forward as though he were a weak mortal man.

He would have to play the game.

He found the thought to be highly invigorating. The woman was a challenge! He had not been truly challenged, particularly by a female, since his own turning. He felt like a boy, beside himself in his own excitement.

The phone on his desk rang in two short bursts, and he picked up the receiver. "This is President DeSai."

"This is Lamb, sir. May I come to your office again?"

DeSai laughed heartily, knowing the time had been set. "You mean you are not here already?"

The line went dead in Lamb's hand, and he made a beeline for the office of the new President of the United States, the Master.

CHAPTER 18

Rasia Engres hung the receiver back onto the cradle of her desk telephone. She sat back in her office chair and considered the appointment she had just made: a one-on-one interview with a US President! Not only would this be good for her career, but it could also be the best thing for her future all the way around.

She did not intend to be a journalist into old age. This was simply her career of choice because she was an exceptionally good communicator and manipulator. She was now head of her department and had her eye on the editor's chair, but she was biding her time. If she played her cards right, she would own this paper within the next five years. She had a plan carefully outlined, and she would do whatever it took to meet her goals.

But she would sleep with no one to gain the advancement she desired. Sex weakened the resolve, and the guts, of everyone. No, it was not an option.

She was suspicious of the new President; the way he looked at her at the press conference was something she was very familiar with. She was strikingly beautiful, and she knew it. He was just another man in the end though, no matter how sexy he was, and he was extraordinarily sexy, but that simply did not matter to her. He would, however, help her personal plan move a lot more smoothly if she could work him right. He could put her where she wanted to be, and where was that, exactly?

She wanted to be in complete control of everything. Who knew? Maybe he would sweep her off her feet and marry her, and she could run America, and thus the world, from the shadows.

Ha! She highly doubted it. She had yet to meet a man of anywhere near that caliber. Rasia simply didn't believe one existed.

But she would take this interview; it could only help. She would go with the flow, but she believed her icy demeanor would repel him quickly if he did not reflect the qualities that would benefit her. She chuckled aloud. How evil she was! How little she cared!

These, in her opinion, were the qualities of a real woman, and she had all of them, and the fact was that luck had nothing to do with it.

She had been blessed with her good looks by both parents. Her mother and father had been incredibly attractive, if not too bright. Once her father died her mother had gone from man to man, looking for someone to take care of her weak-willed self and her beautiful little red-headed daughter. Even at a very young age, these men began to get ideas regarding Rasia.

At the tender age of eleven, she had driven a chef's knife through the heart of her mother's third boyfriend for touching her budding breasts. The memory brought a smile to her face, as did the remembrance of dragging his lifeless body out the back door, across the fenced-in yard, and into the river. Even the recollection of cleaning up the man's blood made her tingle.

Men were pigs, and she had spent a lifetime using them like so much toilet paper, and she had no qualms about disposing of them in much the same way. They were not beings, they were things to Rasia Engres. Here she was, thirty-years-old, and her virginity was still intact. As far as she was concerned, it would stay that way.

At fifteen, she was asked to a dance with a young man from her class at school. He had brought a bottle of cheap wine from the local market to their date, and she was excited about taking a sip or two. They had ducked out of the dance early and walked to a local park to sit by a pond and imbibe a bit. They had each taken only a drink apiece when the advances began.

Initially, she simply shooed him away, but he became more persistent with each drink they took. Her head buzzed nicely, but it did not lessen her judgment. In her frustration with his outrageous behavior, she began to encourage him a bit, and finally, just as she had hoped, he lost control and attempted to force her.

She 'gave in' then, or so it had appeared to him. She offered to take him in her mouth, and he eagerly agreed. Only seconds after she began, she bit down on his manhood so hard it would require a total of eighty stitches to reattach it properly. She told him to leave her name out of it, or she would scream rape.

You see, this had been her plan all along. He was the

editor of the class paper, and she was a mere step below him. She wanted his spot, and later that week, she secured it.

Yes, a beautiful, focused, determined, and a cold individual was Rasia Engres.

That had been the beginning of her 'career.' There were some things she loved about her work; she loved the people she met, the parties she attended, and the travel she was able to indulge in. She would love to be able to focus on these three things without her job being the reason they were in her life.

She could be wrong, and she knew it. There was a good chance that President DeSai really just wanted to give an exclusive interview, and that he had no interest in her at all. No… she doubted it. He would not have remembered her so clearly or singled her out for the privilege without ulterior motives. She was finely tuned into these things; her life experience had made her that way.

So she would fly with her photographer Oleks to interview the President the day after the next. It would be interesting to see how everything played out. It would be even more interesting to learn his vulnerabilities, and if she could use any of them to her advantage.

Funny, but she felt like she had just struck gold.

CHAPTER 19

The moment DeSai found out that he would be giving a face to face interview with Rasia Engres in only two days, he experienced a literal physical rush of relief. This was new to him; tension and concern were part of being a walking dead man. You lived by your wits, and you murdered for nourishment, but now that he was in control, and had seen such success, the feeling he experienced was much like throwing a heavy weight off one's back. He hadn't a care in the world.

During the days before the interview, he walked on air. He was happy, constantly smiling, and took to his new 'position' like a fish to water. Those who 'worked' with him catered to him constantly, and his family was as busy as ever bringing new family members into the fold.

As the Master, sex was a part of their homecoming, with the women anyway. The only thing that he found a bit nerve-racking was the fact that he had no sexual desire, and this was beyond his understanding. The animal in him should be drawn to it, yet when a woman was spread bare before him, he found himself more unimpressed than anything. This culminated the night before the interview.

One of the members of his cabinet, Clifford Cummings, had bitten a beautiful woman of thirty-six. She was an attorney from Amsterdam who was in the States vacationing with friends. He had met her at a dance club in downtown Washington, and luring her with the powers he now had was simple. She had been mesmerized by him, and she couldn't wait to go back to his apartment.

Their sex was steamy and acrobatic; at one point he thought she may kill him, though he knew this would not occur. After their hot, sweaty bodies were spent, she fell asleep next to him quickly. Clifford bit her in a flash, and she didn't even move. He had rolled over and slept himself.

The next day she felt the pull to go to the master, and she found herself standing in front of the white house dazed and confused. While she had no idea what she was doing, she knew she had to do it. She was granted immediate entrance, surprisingly enough, and in no time she was enjoying some of the best wine she had ever had in her life with the President himself.

DeSai had taken her breath away! He was so handsome she couldn't think straight, and the very sound of his voice made her juices flow. She knew she was to sleep with him, just as she instinctively knew that he was in complete control of her, body and soul. What she didn't know was that regardless of her outstanding physical beauty and alluring scent, the thought of sex with her was putting him at ease.

So DeSai tuned out completely. He turned music on loudly so he could not hear her strange accent or the tone of her voice. He kept his eyes tightly closed thinking of Rasia. He didn't even attempt to inflict even the slightest amount of pain on her, for he just wanted to get it done and send her out with his other soldiers. Many in Amsterdam needed to be turned. He even came early in order to end the encounter as quickly as possible, but this was only after she was satisfied, of course. She left his quarters with a happy, zombie-like smile on her face.

He showered as soon as she left, scrubbing her scent from his skin using the hottest of water. He scrubbed himself until his pale white skin was actually red from the pain, and still, he could smell her. She faded only after he closed his eyes picturing Rasia.

Now he lay in bed alone, clean sheets enveloping him. It was one o'clock in the morning, and he would meet Rasia for the interview right after lunch at one in the afternoon. It seemed to him like the appointment was weeks away. He couldn't sleep, but he was building a ravenous appetite for fresh blood. He knew that the blood and only the blood would calm his nervous soul.

That was when he decided to call the luscious Ukrainian reporter himself and thank her for accepting his invitation to interview. He reached into his nightstand and pulled out a folded piece of paper with Rasia's personal cell phone number on it. He felt no apprehension about making the call, but he was nervous that it would provoke her to refuse the interview. It mattered not to him; he had to hear her voice, and he was confident that he could convince her he had only the purest of intentions.

He sat up on the side of his bed and took the telephone receiver off the cradle. He dialed the number almost blindly, then put the phone to his ear. There was a bit of static, then it began to ring.

"Hello."

Cyril sat up straight. "Hello, Ms. Engres?"

"Yes. Who is calling please?" She sounded a bit annoyed, then he realized the time difference. She was likely getting ready to catch her flight! He felt foolish for making the call.

"It is Cyril DeSai calling," he said. "I apologize for bothering you if I have. I forgot the time difference between our locations."

Rasia cleared her throat into the phone. "How can I help you, Mr. President?"

DeSai took a deep breath. "I know we will see each other for the interview soon, but I have been planning the entertainment for you and your photographer, as well as the meals. I just wondered if you have any preferences food-wise?"

"You called me to ask me what I like to eat?"

Now Cyril felt a bit foolish. It did seem silly that he would phone her at the last minute to ask about her culinary tastes. "I was simply curious if you had preferences. Do you like wine? If so, what is your favorite?"

"Mr. President," Rasia began, clearly annoyed. "I

don't care what you serve for food, as we were not planning on socializing with you during this visit. As for wine, I adore it. If you want to indulge me, I prefer a nice rich Shiraz, but anything red will do."

DeSai felt a bit alarmed at her admission that she and her photographer did not plan on dining with him. He had arranged for a three day stay for the pair so he could get to know her. He would have to manipulate this situation quickly and efficiently.

"I do apologize again for disturbing you. It is my hope you will reconsider my invitation to dine. My kitchen staff has gone to great lengths to prepare for your visit," he said with remorse.

She cleared her throat once again, but this time it sounded more like a growl. "I am preparing to catch my flight," she said curtly. "I do not see me changing my mind, but I am sure this could be better discussed tomorrow."

"Yes, yes," he began. "I simply wanted to see to it that you would want for nothing while visiting."

"This is not a social call, President," she replied harshly.

Cyril nodded in the darkness of his room. "I understand, but the comfort of even professional guests is important to me."

Rasia was quiet, so Cyril awkwardly continued. "So, I guess I will see you tomorrow afternoon, then?"

The woman still did not reply. "Hello?" DeSai persisted.

Rasia Engres had hung up.

Now he smiled broadly. What a vixen! She woke a desire for blood in him that came in waves. It was time for him to get his anxiety out. He needed to feed.

Cyril rose quickly and dressed in his traditional black colors. He picked up the telephone on the bedside stand and requested that his limousine is prepared; he wanted to take a drive into the countryside. He planned to quench his thirst in one way or another as soon as possible, and since the entirety of his staff was family now, he knew he could do so with no problem at all.

If he couldn't find a human, and their numbers were dwindling, any animal would do. It was simply the blood and the peace it always brought that he needed. He needed to completely take a life and put that life inside of himself.

He entered the limo through the hidden garage, which had been built for the safety of former presidents. He did not need this now; nearly the entire nation belonged to him. He would use it, though. It was always important to keep up appearances, at least until he was able to safely say that not just the nation, but the world belonged to him as well.

He directed the driver to head into the country, and soon the lights of the city were far behind him. He would feel the presence of a human that had not yet turned, and he would smell an animal. If they had not found someone within an hour of driving, he would take the first scent that came his way.

But as it turned out he had nothing to be concerned about. They were only fifteen minutes out of town when he felt a man. He told his driver to pull the limo over. "I'm going to walk a minute, and I will not need an escort."

He climbed from the large vehicle and walked to its rear, where he raised his arms into the air and swiftly took flight into the night sky. Oh, his new life had robbed him of this pleasure! The feeling of the wind in his face gave him overwhelming pleasure. He would not have made a different decision this night, and soon he would do it again. He had forgotten that this was as much a part of who and what he was as the drive to 'procreate' his species by building a family.

He flew about a quarter of a mile, following the sense of energy he had picked up from the nearby male human. There were no houses here; this person was holed up somewhere outside. He could see as if it were daylight, and in a short time, he saw him, trudging up the road in a ragged oversized coat.

He wasted no time. He swooped down on the man, who didn't even know what hit him.

"Ugh!" This was the only sound the bum made when DeSai took him. He landed with the man in his arms, struggling slightly, in a nearby culvert, and brought his mouth to the man's jugular in one blurred movement.

He drank as though he were dying of thirst; not even a drop dripped down his chin. The man reeked of sweat and urine almost overbearingly, especially for a species which depended on their sense of smell for so many things, but the satisfaction he experienced from the man's lifeblood intoxicated him, and soon the terrible odor which emanated from him became all but non-existent to Cyril DeSai.

He sucked so eagerly that he nearly choked, and he continued with gusto long after the life flew from the man's shell of a body. DeSai let his spent flesh drop to the ground, used up. He looked at the man with disgust; he had served his purpose, and he could have never been a productive, lasting member of his family, so this was meant to be.

He was energized and immediately took the sky, soaring and dashing about in the air, playing like a child. He spun and zipped to and fro with great passion, and finally, he headed back to the waiting limousine with its driver and Secret Service agent.

When he arrived, he gave his mouth a lick to ensure he hadn't gotten his 'food' on his face, and then he opened the car door and sat down with hardly a sound.

"Take me back home."

The car took off right away, and in no time, they were headed back to the bright lights of Washington, D.C.

CHAPTER 20

Rasia Engres stood before a mirror in the ladies' room at Reagan National Airport freshening her makeup and straightening her clothing. The flight in from Kiev had seemed unbearable, not to mention uncharacteristically long. She had spent the entire night before her flight, as well as the flight itself, considering how Cyril DeSai could be used to her advantage, and as time had passed, she found herself getting more and more excited at the prospects.

His call early this morning as she had been preparing to go to the airport had infuriated her. Who did the man think he was, anyway? She didn't care if he was the king of the Earth, he was nothing more to her than an opportunity, at least as far as he knew. How dare he call her personal telephone?

Rasia possessed a murderous rage inside of her, and this she knew full well. It was what had driven her most of her life. Hatred and anger were nourishment to her, and while she was capable of killing a soul without batting an eye, she knew she was not suited for prison or death row. She controlled her sick thoughts and twisted appetites by exercising her evils in her day to day life, and thus far this had proven to suffice. All other indulgences were carried out by her very secretly, and she was a very good planner.

She left the restroom area through the hordes of women around her, her heels clicking on the tiles of the floor loudly for a place with so much noise. She made it into the main concourse, where she had disembarked, and looked around for her cameraman Oleks. He had gone to relieve himself as well, and now they needed to gather their bags and find a taxi as soon as possible; after all, they were to meet DeSai at the White House in three short hours, and they still needed to check into their hotel.

She took her cell phone out of her bag and turned it on, then looked around the area directly in front of the men's room and in only a few moments, she spotted the young man looking dazed; he was looking for her as well, and all the people had the poor idiot confused. She made her way toward him waving her arm and calling his name; finally, she captured his attention, and a look of relief spread over his face as he wormed through the crowd and headed to meet her.

Right then her cell rang. Rasia stopped and looked at the display. It was the same number DeSai had called her from earlier! The man was indeed determined, and this gave her much to consider. It could be information that would work in her favor in the end, for sure. She was onto the new American president, little did he know. She silenced the phone and dropped it into her bag before turning her attention to Oleks.

"We need to get our bags and other equipment, then get a cab to the hotel as quickly as possible. We have no time to waste, so you head for the baggage carousel, and I will meet you there in a moment; I am going to call the hotel to double check on our reservations," she told him, and off he went. She stepped out of the main line of traffic and made the call; all was ready and waiting for them.

By the time she was finished making her phone calls, she had spotted Oleks coming toward her from the baggage carousel. He had all the bags they had checked, and the big oaf was juggling them very nicely. She smiled to herself. See, men had some kind of purpose after all.

The hotel had informed her that the reservations she had made for their rooms were put on hold by none other than the President himself. He had paid for two rooms for a total of three nights. While hearing this made her blood boil, she kept herself under control. She didn't care what DeSai wanted. This was her game, and it would remain hers alone.

When the two stepped outside, the first thing she saw was a single limo situated amongst the fleet of taxicabs. DeSai had even presumed to send transport! Rasia took Oleks by the arm and steered him away from it so he would not see her name on the large white card the driver was holding. They would get a cab anyway.

It took no time to obtain a cab, as taxis were lined up along the curb at the main entrance. Within a half-hour, they were standing at the desk at the hotel, where

Rasia was informed once again that the bill, and all charges, were to be covered by President Cyril DeSai. They need not even show a credit card or identification.

She was impressed with her room, as she was sure Oleks would be, but her shallow little mind could not help but wonder how much better things would be in one, five, or ten years. Surely, if things went her way, they would be even better than this. She unpacked her bag, as they would stay three full nights and enjoy the area a bit, and once she was finished, she changed her clothes. For the interview, she chose a pink satin collared button-down blouse, a brown fitted blazer with pink pinstripes, and a matching pencil skirt. She joined this with a pair of brown and pink heels and her signature scent. She wore her waist-length red hair up off her neck in a very sophisticated style, and once her makeup was fresh, she stood back and looked in the mirror.

"Knock 'em dead," she told her reflection with a satisfied sneer.

After meeting Oleks in the corridor, they headed to the lobby, where the exact same limo and driver was waiting for them, courtesy of Cyril DeSai. This man is really on top of his game, Rasia thought. She realized the driver was probably given a description of her, maybe even shown a picture. It pleased her to think that he watched her snub the ride he was there to provide. She wondered what the President had thought when he received a call telling him that she and her photographer had gotten into a cab at the airport. She hoped he had been as annoyed as she was regarding his calls to her phone.

"The President, Cyril DeSai, welcomes you to Washington, Ms. Engres. Shall I put your bags in the trunk for safekeeping?" He was very prim and proper, but he was sure to greet her with a smile. Neither his voice nor the look on his face said anything about her rejection at the airport.

She smiled stiffly in return. "Yes, that would be perfect. Oleks, you can board on the other side of the vehicle."

Her young cameraman jumped and then headed to the door on the driver's side of the limousine, which he soon disappeared inside of. Rasia waited for the driver to open her door for her. She was going to make them all work for whatever it was DeSai was aiming to get. May as well take advantage of the good things in life, especially when they are free. Life is way too short as it is.

Once inside the limo, the driver put up the glass divider and proceeded to make his way out of the chaotic driveway area. Rasia didn't skip a beat. She began to look through the wet bar, and finally chose a small single serving bottle of Cabernet Sauvignon by Cliffside Wineries. After sampling its aroma for a moment, her eyebrows raised; not bad at all. She was impressed, and she was also glad she had brought breath mints.

Oleks reached for the bar himself, and Rasia slapped his hand as though he were a toddler trying to get a cookie. "Use your brain, moron. We're going to meet President DeSai. I need you on your toes at all times." Oleks cowered back in his seat and began to pout as he stared out the window of the limo.

They reached the White House at twelve-thirty. Rasia had anticipated all kinds of red tape regarding being granted entry, but the Secret Service men who met them in the underground garage didn't even bother to search their belongings; they were simply escorted into the main house by the men, who seemed to be anxious to deliver them to the Oval Office.

She and Oleks walked between the two men during the stroll, and as they made their way into the heart of the president's home, Rasia turned to Oleks, and with a sneer said to him, "You realize I'm on my way, don't you?"

∞

Cyril DeSai was nervous. He could not remember the last time he was aware of actual nerves, but they were sharp today. He was even fidgeting. He had been notified when Rasia and her cameraman arrived, and he knew that they were on their way to him, even now. It didn't help that he felt like a schoolboy regarding having called the woman's cell twice. What had he been thinking?

They were still five minutes from arriving when his nose picked up her luscious scent, and it caused him to groan; he even got an erection from her smell and had to rush into the bathroom and douse himself with cold water to control the thing. There was seriously something about this woman, something… tangible. He knew deep inside of him that Rasia was the one. Never before in all his centuries had he such a violent reaction to the presence of a female.

He was just closing the bathroom door when the knock came. He straightened himself out quickly and strode back to his desk. It would not be acceptable to let Ms. Engres see him so shaken. No, not acceptable at all.

He had dressed just for her on this occasion. He wore traditional black, but his suit was cut with Asian styling, and he wore a blood red satin tie. It was his favorite color, after all.

"Enter, please," he said. He never used the word please; he viewed it as weak, but he thought it was a nice touch today.

The door opened and the Secret Service man who had opened it stood to the side and said, "Rasia Engres and Oleksandre Vanderflute, Mr. President."

DeSai made his way toward them, his hands extended in a warm, welcoming gesture. He made a point of taking the hand of the fresh-faced cameraman first; he had already appeared overly anxious. He was determined to control himself around Rasia Engres from then on. Now Cyril took notice that her escort was no more than a boy. As a chaperone he only filled the third seat, intruding on potential privacy. Certainly, he was good for nothing else!

"Mr. Vanderflute, it is wonderful to make your acquaintance," DeSai began, taking the young man's right hand in both of his own. "Thank you for coming. I hope you have found your accommodations to be comfortable and pleasing."

Oleks flushed. "Yes, Mr. President," he said, his voice trembling. "They are quite beautiful, thank you."

With that nonsense out of the way, Cyril turned his attention to Rasia; his stomach jumped inside of him. She was ten times more beautiful than he recalled from their brief and distant encounter during the press conference. DeSai had to force himself not to freeze up; he was smitten! He took her hand in both of his and raised it to his lips, and he planted a soft, gentle kiss there.

"Ms. Engres, it is my pleasure to see you again."

Rasia was satisfied. Yes, this was more than an interview with this man; his eyes were on fire for her. He was the 'one,' and he would make an easy target. If she did this right, he could take her further than she ever imagined.

She pulled her hand firmly from his grasp and, hardening her voice ever so slightly, said, "Likewise, I'm sure, Mr. President. Now shall we get down to business?"

With that, he offered them two seats, and they sat, Oleks getting his gear ready and Rasia preparing a handheld recorder. She was cold and about as far from him as any woman he could ever remember. She was a conquest; she was perfect.

Cyril DeSai would never be the same again.

CHAPTER 21

"What would you like to drink?" Cyril asked as they shuffled around. "On the table before you, there is about every beverage imaginable. Please, help yourselves."

Rasia looked up and offered him a tight smile. "President DeSai, acquiring the presidency of the most powerful and abundant nation on Earth must be quite an achievement. How do you feel now that you are in office?" asked Rasia Engres.

DeSai smiled at her. She was a tough one, and here he was, feeling like a nervous adolescent.

"It is invigorating. While I am aware of the weight of the responsibility I now hold, I am also aware of all of the great people I am surrounded with, and together I am confident that I will serve a highly successful term," he replied.

She nodded vaguely. "What state are you from?"

"I was born in France; my parents were French winemakers, as were theirs before them, and theirs, so I come from a long line of vintners. My ancestors all hail from France," he said. "Where do you originally come from, Rasia?"

She made eye contact with him briefly and then ignored the question altogether. "Your administration seems to have rallied behind you like none in the past have managed to do. What do you attribute this to… sir?"

He immediately noticed her hesitation at the use of this formal address, and he could smell the defiance in her attitude. It made her more striking than ever, and once again his erection began to grow; it pressed uncomfortably against the fabric of his silk trousers. He was glad to be behind his desk.

"I attribute it to the fact that I treat each and every individual in this administration as if they were my family. I do not see in black and white, so the silliness of parties is a waste of time, in my opinion. We are all human beings here, are we not?"

Oleks had stood and was taking a series of rapid shots, moving around the room to get varying perspectives. DeSai had completely forgotten that the boy existed. Rasia, on the other hand, found herself more thankful than ever for his presence. She was putting on a good show, but DeSai had her full attention. Her heart was even pounding a bit, but she maintained a rigid façade.

The interview continued in this way for two full hours. While it seemed that Rasia Engres was trying to trip him up, she was really just getting to know him, putting up her antennas for any weak spot he may have in his confident armor. While Cyril appeared confident and self-assured, his hands were trembling beneath his desk, and he was using them to control his unruly penis.

At the end of the interview, both Rasia and Oleks began to pack up their equipment, and it seemed to Cyril that she was going to slip through his fingers once again. She showed absolutely no interest in getting to know him personally, but he, on the other hand, could not erase the vision of her from his mind.

"Mr. President," Oleks said, speaking for the first time since the interview had begun, "Where is a restroom that I could use, please sir?"

Rasia's eyes flashed toward the antsy cameraman, and it did not escape DeSai's notice. He turned to Oleks, smiling pleasantly. "Of course, of course. Just go left into the corridor. You will find it past the main staircase, about five doors down." Cyril kept the knowledge of his own personal facilities to himself. This was an opportunity to sneak a moment with Rasia.

Rasia's eyes followed the man as he left the office. "Hurry back, Oleks. I am ready to return to the hotel and work on writing this piece."

When Cyril realized that it was her full intention to leave immediately, he jumped into action. "Ms. Engres, your room is covered for the next three days, and we could take care of it for a longer period, if you like," Cyril said, controlling the eagerness in his voice just barely. "You should spend some time in the city and visit some of our sites. I would be thrilled if you would allow me the pleasure of showing you around," Rasia stopped packing her attaché case and looked him in the eye. "I have been to this city many times, Mr.

President."

"Yes, Ms. Engres, but I am sure there are things I could show you which you have never before seen."

Their eyes locked and he felt the fire; it was tangible and wholly intoxicating, and he knew by the look on her face that she felt it too. He had to act fast. "We could have an early dinner now, or cocktails, and simply chat."

She resumed packing, not answering him immediately. He didn't push her, but when she was finished, she met his gaze once again. When she finally spoke, he could detect the slight strain in her voice from controlling her own tone.

"We may take you up on that. What did you have in mind?"

He thought fast. "Well, I know that you like to have Mr. Vanderflute in your company, so I am willing to have him along. We could eat at a wonderful little steak house I like to frequent; we would have the entire place to ourselves. Afterward, or even before for that matter, I could take you to my winery, Cliffside, and give you the grand tour. I think a woman like yourself would appreciate all that can be gleaned from such a business."

It was as if DeSai had known what the magic words would be; Rasia had a passion for fine wine and fancied herself somewhat of a connoisseur. "When did you want to do this... sir?"

How he loved her stubbornness. She would need to be taught to submit, but he would have an eternity to teach her. He replied, "When is a good time for you? We could do it tomorrow, and the two of you could have dinner here now before you leave."

Already DeSai had one of his finest females arranged for Oleks, for when they did finally return to their quarters. She simply needed to get him while he was away from Rasia, but Rasia was proving to be tougher than he thought she would be. He had attempted to mesmerize her with his tantalizing power, with his eyes, but she would not give. It seemed she was immune, and this sparked an even greater love and desire than he had thought possible within him.

"Hmmm. We could eat here. Where should we store our things?" She was beginning to melt just a little, DeSai thought.

He quickly responded by pressing a button on an intercom unit on his desk. "Mr. Lamb, would you please come and take Mr. Vanderflute's and Ms. Engres' bags into the main coat room? They will be taking their meal with us."

In what seemed like seconds, there was a light knock on the office door, and a young man with a bit of acne entered the office. He took the bags they handed him, bowed slightly in DeSai's direction, and left.

"Your staff seems very dedicated to someone who is a newly elected official, Mr. DeSai. You must be very good to them," said Rasia. The power he had over those around him was obvious to her. The behavior they demonstrated before this man was not simply respect. No, it was… worship. Like a slave to a master…

He smiled a genuine smile at the journalist. "As I have said, they are family to me, and I make sure they know it."

The three made their way out of the office, and Cyril DeSai led his future queen and her post-adolescent cameraman in the direction of the dining hall.

∞

The White House chef had prepared a succulent meal, as always, which included an appetizer of crab and scallop cakes with a jalapeño tartar, a simple dinner salad, grilled swordfish in lemon butter served on a bed of angel hair pasta, steamed green beans with sesame, almond, and parmesan, and seasoned roasted red baby potatoes. For dessert, he had prepared banana bread pudding with white chocolate sauce.

They all ate together in silence initially. It was not until the dinner salad was served that Cyril overcame his nerves and started the conversation. Rasia was evasive, and Oleks was bumbling before him. He knew he must take matters into his own hands and get the ball rolling while he had a chance.

"Rasia, is your family in Kiev?" Cyril began things by staying basic. It wouldn't do to scare her off now.

She wiped her mouth with her napkin. "President, I don't typically share much about myself during professional meetings."

Cyril kept the smile on his face, but he was beginning to see the inside of his being. "You know, dear, not more than ninety minutes ago, I was telling you all the graphic details of my life, and you cannot share one?"

Rasia took notice that his smile remained, but there

was an undertone to his voice that did not match. A chill ran up her spine; this man had used a tone of slight authority with her! Never had anyone ever really dared to do that, and it was very alluring to her indeed.

She smiled at him and then lifted her glass of chilled Chardonnay to her lips. With a slight smile, she replied, "I suppose just one."

Now Cyril could feel it: she was coming around. He knew that it had nothing to do with mesmerizing her with his eyes. He also knew that something in him was touching something in her, and it was a sensation he could not put into words.

"So, is your family in Kiev then?" DeSai lightened his voice significantly with this statement. He adjusted himself in his chair so he could give her his full attention.

Rasia put down her napkin and wine glass and sat back in her chair, her elbows resting on the armrests. "I have no living family. I was an only child, and both of my parents are dead."

"Yes," Cyril said. "Mine are as well."

The room grew still, and the trio turned their attention back to their salads. After a couple of bites, Oleks surprised everyone by speaking out. "Mr. President, I just wanted to tell you what an honor it is to meet you and dine with you."

Rasia threw the young man a look of surprise before Cyril responded. "It is my pleasure, Oleks." Now he turned toward the cameraman. "Tell me, do you have a wife? Children?"

Oleks blushed and shook his head, looking down at his plate. "No, sir. I'm not ready for that. With work I…"

"Oleks doesn't currently have a lot of time for extracurricular activities," Rasia interrupted. "I am somewhat of a slave driver, as I'm sure he would tell you if I were not present."

Now Cyril laughed out loud, and the other two joined him. Rasia had just made an attempt at humor, though it hadn't worked out for her too well. Oleks looked completely panic-stricken by her comment, but Cyril had seen the laughter in her eyes.

He found he wanted to know everything about her, and she had put a distance between the two of them, but he felt the gap narrowing ever so slowly. He decided that if he wanted her to stay for at least three days, he would have to take things very slowly. Not bombard her with questions that were too much, too fast.

At the end of the meal, they were offered coffee or brandy, and while Cyril and Oleks had the brandy, Rasia stuck with coffee. She was not about to get even the slightest bit loose now. The food served here was nothing like anything she had ever eaten in her life; her host had exquisite taste, and the power he had come to suited his entire personality. He was sexy and loaded with charisma, and something about his eyes seemed to daze her. More than once she literally had to force herself to look away from him; his gaze made her feel powerless and powerless was something she had long ago determined she would not allow herself to feel.

This man was a catch, and love had absolutely nothing to do with it. When it came to Rasia Engres, she wanted something only if it meant her own personal gain. Her interest in President Cyril DeSai was based solely on this.

At least it had been. She had a nagging feeling in the back of her mind that at some point during the meal something had shifted for her. She caught herself looking at him out of the corner of her eye just to admire him when he was talking to Oleks. She had scolded herself, then caught herself doing it twice more.

But she would not let herself lose control. There was still way too much to learn about the man personally before she would even consider kissing him. But she was already certain that he stood out from all other men she had ever met, and in more ways than one.

As for DeSai, he knew that he was in dangerous territory with Rasia Engres, but he was sure that he would take the upper hand on the situation. He needed only to make her fully his first. Love, he thought. What was love like? He remembered love as an emotion, but he had not felt it in literally hundreds of years, not since Cecile. He had always assumed, at least ever since that fated night when he was turned, that love was not something that could be experienced by his species, and he had allowed his instincts and appetites to drive him ever since. Now, though, he was beginning to strongly reconsider. The fact of the matter was that Rasia had him in mental and emotional knots. He would do what it took to win her over.

"So, Ms. Engres, would you like to see some of Washington with me tomorrow, as we discussed in my office?" He was eager, but his voice did not give this fact away. His eyes were another matter altogether, though. He held them fast on her, wanting to take in everything about her response.

She took a sip of her coffee and looked him fully in the eyes. She felt the gooseflesh rise up on her skin, and it took her by surprise. She said, "You know, I don't allow myself to mix my profession with my personal life, Mr. President. I have mentioned this on several occasions, both to you and Mr. Lamb." He knew that the words she spoke were an act, to keep up appearances. She was going to give in, he just knew it deep inside. "I am not trying to be rude, but it is a life rule I have always lived by." She looked away from him and sipped her coffee once again.

She was playing cat and mouse; he saw it on her face, and just then, for the first time, he noticed that she squirmed a bit under his look. This was very good, and he was glad she had lost her bearings slightly.

He smiled just a bit and took a sip of his own brandy. After glancing at Oleks, he said, "Your friend here is welcome to join us, and you're going to be here three days, after all." He looked directly at her and continued. "You're a focused, driven woman. Wouldn't you agree that never treating one's self to rest and relaxation every so often instigates future ineffectiveness?"

Now she met his eyes with her own. "I would

venture to agree, yes. Sure, President. I would be honored to accompany you around your city tomorrow. I am very tired now, however. I think Oleks and I will be leaving. What time should I arrive here tomorrow?"

"You won't need to 'arrive'; the driver will pick you up." He couldn't take his eyes off of her, and his stomach felt nervous and shaky; he rose from his chair and held his hand out to help Rasia to her feet. She took it but kept her eyes averted from his face.

"Thank you both for dining with me this evening. I look forward to the pleasure of your company tomorrow," he said. "I'll have my driver pick you up at eleven if that suits you, and we can have lunch before we hit the town."

They began walking to the main foyer, and suddenly, the two Secret Service men seemed to appear out of nowhere. "Mr. Dukes, Mr. Reinhardt, please see that Ms. Engres and Mr. Vanderflute get to the car. Tomorrow then?" He looked into Rasia's eyes, and she returned his gaze. He then took her hand and kissed it gently, letting his lips linger for just a moment against her soft flesh. Then he abruptly straightened, and with a smile and nod, he turned on his heel and retreated quickly in the direction of his office.

When they were in the limousine Rasia spoke to Oleks. "The food was delicious, wouldn't you agree?"

"I'd be crazy not to," he replied.

She looked out the window. "Well, you may as well take the evening and find something to do you enjoy. Don't venture about the town, though. You wouldn't want to spoil tomorrow by touring it too soon."

"Thanks. I'm sure I can find something without going too far at all," Oleks said. "If I go out, I intend to only have a drink or two."

Rasia gave him a sideways glance. "Yes, only a drink or two. It wouldn't do for you to be lagging tomorrow, now would it?"

∞

Once she was in her room, Rasia took to her journal and wrote about the afternoon and the interview itself. She filled a full ten pages, front and back, with her recollections and even detailed her thoughts about how Cyril was going to be of great benefit to her future.

She also took a bit of time for personal reflection. She had to admit that, as a man, DeSai had gotten her attention. All her life she had been looking for someone just like him. He couldn't fit the bill better. What had her thrown off was the emotion that he had stirred in her. After a bit of thought, she wrote it off to being a virtual spinster, a virgin at thirty. That was it; she encountered a man who had her attention, and she was horny for the first time in her life. Well, he certainly wouldn't be getting that.

The bottom line was this: she was simply evil, evil to the core, and it was a characteristic about herself that she admired greatly. Rasia Engres was not about to let any man, particularly this one, take that away from her.

∞

Oleks Vanderflute showered and dressed, humming

to himself as he went. He intended to start his evening by having a couple of drinks in the hotel bar, and maybe he would take a short stroll around the block. Ms. Engres was right; he didn't want to ruin the fun tomorrow by taking in too much of the area. He didn't want to spoil the good time they were sure to have with the President.

He left his room around seven-thirty and went to the bar, where he ordered a whiskey and Coke. There were only a handful of people there: a couple of men in business suits sat at the bar, a pair of women had one table, and a single female sat alone at another. Jazz pumped out of the speakers softly, and the lighting was fairly dim.

He had just ordered his second drink when another woman walked in. She sat next to him at the bar and ordered a dry martini with no olives. As the bartender made her drink, she turned to Oleks.

"I just love jazz, don't you?"

At first, he didn't realize she was speaking to him. After all, she wasn't the type women he usually sat next to and began a conversation with. He was sort of a lumbering fellow, and his sense of style was a bit off.

"Yes," he replied. "I would have to say it is one of my favorite genres."

She smiled at him as the bartender set her drink in front of her. She took a credit card from her small clutch and handed it to him. "Keep my tab open, please."

She turned back to Oleks. "I take it you are here on

business?"

"What makes you think so?" he asked.

The woman chuckled softly. "Well, not too many people visiting this fair city stay here unless they are here on business, and I must say, you don't look like a wild, party animal rich boy."

"Okay, you got me," he said, smiling back at her. "My name's Oleks."

"I'm Lucinda. Nice to meet you, Oleks."

She had short blond hair, and it was cut in a style that was very becoming of her small features. Her cheekbones were high and prominent, and her eyes were as blue as the sky. Oleks felt his heart go pitter-patter.

They spent the next two hours drinking and talking, and Oleks was getting a very nice buzz before he knew it. Soon, he was laughing at her jokes, and even tried to make a few of his own. She laughed, but even as his head swam, he knew they weren't funny. The woman was sweeping him off his feet.

"So, Oleks, you have a room here, I take it?" She asked the question while staring him hard in the face, her voice serious now, and very husky.

He couldn't believe it; he was going to get lucky! While Oleks Vanderflute wasn't a virgin, this was not something that happened to him every day. He had managed to sleep with two girls while he was in college, but on both occasions, the girls had been smashed drunk out of their minds. It was only the fact that he wasn't that he had even been able to take advantage of the situations then. Now he was catching a very nice drunk, and he was certain she was as well. He only hoped he could perform.

"I do. Do you?"

She nodded. "Would you like to see my room, Oleks?"

He couldn't accept fast enough, and after they paid for their drinks, the two left the bar, Lucinda holding onto Oleks' arm as they walked out the door.

Her room was on the fifth floor, and it was much smaller than the room the President had gotten for him. He took a seat in one of the chairs and watched her as she turned on some music.

"Would you like a drink?" she asked him.

He nodded at her and then continued to watch her as she made a couple of vodka tonics from the small mini-bar. She moved like a cat, with grace and confidence. She exuded sex, and this was something that had him on the edge of his seat.

Soon she brought him his drink, and when he took it from her, their fingers touched, giving him gooseflesh all over. She set her own drink down on the table and leaned over and kissed him lightly on the lips. Then she kissed him again, this time with more intent, and her tongue found its way into his mouth; he quickly returned the favor, and she began to suck on his.

After a moment she stood and smiled at him, then she walked to the bed and sat down on the foot of it. She patted the spot next to her, inviting him to join her. He didn't even think twice; he jumped up and moved to the bed immediately.

Now they began to kiss with passion. Oleks' head was swimming; he could not believe how lucky he was! Her hands were running up and down his body, and she was pressing herself against the full length of him. In only seconds, he had a raging hard-on, and he wasn't sure he was going to be able to hold off.

As if she had read his mind, she began to unbutton his trousers. They soon dropped to the floor around his ankles, and his underwear soon joined them. She stepped back and took her clothes off quickly; she wore nothing but a dress, and when she took that off, Oleks saw she wore no bra or panties underneath.

She pushed him down on the bed, and he lay on his back with a huge smile on his face as she wrapped her lips around his manhood. Oh, Wow, he thought. If she kept that up too long, he wasn't going to be able to last at all. This was the first time a woman had bestowed this particular favor on him, and he was not at all experienced enough to control himself.

She didn't take him all the way. After a bit, she straddled him and guided him inside of her warm body, and after riding him for only a second Oleks body gave a violent jerk, and he came inside her with great force. She continued to move up and down on him rhythmically until he was spent, at which time she lay on top of him and began to kiss his neck.

Suddenly Lucinda bit him, and she did not do this softly.

"Ouch!" he yelled, but she did not stop. As a matter

of fact, she bit even harder, and he tried to pull away. It seemed he had no strength though, or else she was much stronger than he because she held him fast to the mattress. Now she was sucking at the spot on his neck, and it didn't seem to hurt so much anymore.

He began to get dizzy. "Lucinda... I..." his voice trailed off, and his vision began to get dark around the edges. Those were the last words Oleks would ever speak.

After ten minutes, Lucinda stood and looked down at the dead man who lay on her bed. The job was done. The President's men would be here soon to dispose of the cameraman's body. She wiped her mouth and smiled. He would reward her richly for a job well done, and she didn't even waste much of her evening.

∞

Cyril DeSai had a strong focus on eliminating the cameraman from the equation, and after spending a bit of time with him at dinner, he knew getting rid of the young man completely was the only way to go. He was a bumbling sort so it would be easy, and this was also the reason he had no interest in turning him. Just erase him from the page and get it over with; that was the best way.

He also knew that Oleks, for all his oafishness, would not be an asset worth saving when it came to his purpose. What good would he do Cyril or even the rest of the growing family for that matter? If things didn't work out with Rasia, he would have this fat, unattractive cameraman on his hands who wouldn't even be able to bring him, fresh women. Yes, he was better off gone entirely.

DeSai chose Lucinda only because she had been a whore prior to her turning, and she would know just what to say and do to win the kid over in a very short time. She did her job well. He got the call from her telling him it was finished after only a few short hours, and this pleased him to no end. He directed his two regular servicemen to go take care of the body right away, and then he retired to his room for the night.

Now he would be able to spend the day alone with Rasia, and the oaf Oleks would not be a third wheel. Yes, one has to go to great lengths to get what one wants, but it would be worth it in the end. Cyril was sure of this.

CHAPTER 22

Rasia Engres rose at six o'clock, the next morning and took a long, leisurely shower after she ordered her breakfast from room service. She intended to spend the next four hours putting together her piece for the 'Post' on President DeSai. Today was sure to give her more material yet so she wouldn't get too carried away, but she wanted to turn in something outstanding. She wanted it to be personal, and she wanted it to pack a punch. No one else would be able to top her, and this would be the first piece about the brand new American president to hit newsstands.

She stepped out of the shower and dried off, then wrapped a towel around her wet hair, making a turban out of it. Her mind went to Oleks. She would call his room and have him bring her his camera so she could watch the digital recordings and pick some stills out of it if she wasn't satisfied with the stills he had already chosen. Certainly, he was up and working.

There was a knock on the door as she exited the bathroom. She answered it in her bathrobe and took the tray of food from the hands of the maid in the hall. She then went to her purse to get a tip for the girl before shutting the door and locking it.

Now she sat at the table with her breakfast before her and picked up the phone to call Oleks' room. She dialed, but all she got was a dull ringing on the other end. He must be in the shower.

After twenty minutes she tried again, and when she didn't get an answer, she dialed his cell phone. He didn't answer that either. Now she was getting pissed. Oleks Vanderflute knew that he was supposed to be at her beck and call; he was lucky she had let him have a bit of time to himself last night, and now he was taking advantage. It was breaking into her work, and this was something she would not accept.

She got up in a huff and threw on a pair of jeans and a t-shirt. After slipping a pair of loafers on her feet, she grabbed the key card to her room and walked out into the corridor. She was so worked up that she paid no attention to the number on the door before knocking, and she was greeted by a woman of about sixty at the first one.

The woman looked Rasia over. "Can I help you?"

"Sorry, wrong room," she said, without so much as a smile. Now she walked to the other door and began to pound on it, yelling his name. He did not answer.

"Oleks! Did you get drunk? Wake up!" There was not so much as a sound coming from the other side of the door, not even the television he loved to watch so much. She took the elevator down to the lobby and approached the front desk.

"Good morning. My cameraman is in the room next

to mine, and I think he may have gotten a bit tipsy last night. I can't wake him, and we have work to do. Could I have the key to his room, please?" She asked. Her voice was pleasant, but there was a sneer on her face.

"What room, madame?" asked the clerk.

"Room 435," she replied.

After he punched some numbers into a small machine, he swiped a key card through it and handed it to her with a smile. "The President called this morning to check on your well-being. He said to tell you his driver would be waiting for you out front at eleven sharp."

"Thank you," she said, and turned and walked back to the elevator.

When Rasia arrived at Oleks' door, she didn't even bother to knock first; she was furious now. She keyed the door with the card, and it immediately popped open. She stepped in and flipped the light switch to the left of the door.

The bed was still made. He had not even slept there the night before.

It took a moment for the cleanliness and emptiness of the room to take root in her mind, and she stood staring at the bed incredulously. "Screw it," she finally said, and she walked over and grabbed his camera case and then left the room, slamming the door behind her.

Back in her own room, she began to view the video, tapping the screen to create the still shots she wanted. She worked on this for an hour before settling down to outline her article. She was going to produce a true

masterpiece, and she was getting more and more excited
with each passing minute.

At ten, she began to pull out of her work-induced
trance a bit, and she knew it was time to start getting
ready to meet President DeSai. She tried Oleks on his
cell again and then she changed into a yellow sundress
with matching flats. She tried him again and then put on
her makeup, making sure it was flawless. She tried him
yet again but to no avail. Now she brushed her long,
wavy red locks; she would wear her hair down today.

Normally she would not even consider meeting a
man without her companion; this would usually
eliminate the chances of him hitting on her; after all, she
wasn't going to give in, and advances always just made
things awkward. But today, she would be meeting the
President on her own. It would be fine; didn't he always
have secret service with him anyway?

At ten minutes to eleven, she strode off the elevator
and walked through the lobby. She could see the
President's limousine waiting, and the driver was
standing at the rear door.

"Good morning, Ms. Engres, I hope you were able
to get plenty of rest," he greeted her as he opened the
door for her.

She nodded curtly at him. "Yes, thank you," she
replied as she got into the back of the limo.

Soon, they were pulling into the underground garage
at the White House, and Rasia found herself wondering
what kind of wonderful food he would feed her for
lunch. Her stomach was growling, and she was more

than ready to have a bite.

She had tried Oleks many times during the drive, to no avail. With each unsuccessful attempt, she had grown angrier, and now it was time to put on her professional face. She had to push the thought of her absent and missing cameraman out of her mind.

Secret Service met her inside and escorted her to the dining room, where Cyril DeSai sat waiting, a smile across his face.

"Hello, Ms. Engres! You look luminous. Yellow is definitely your color," he began, standing and pulling her chair out so she could sit. "Where is Mr. Vanderflute? Did he need to use the facilities?"

Rasia looked at him as he sat back down. "No, he decided he wouldn't be joining us today. Normally, I would have canceled because of his decision, but you have gone to the trouble of planning the day, so here I am." She took a drink from the water glass at her place.

"Well, I'm certainly glad you didn't. I would have been deeply disappointed," Cyril said. As if on cue, a servant came into the dining room with a tray holding two bowls of soup, both flanked by chunks of steaming bread.

The servant placed the bowls in front of them, then turned to Rasia. "The soup is our bisque of tomato and lobster. What would you have to drink, Madame?"

"I would enjoy a glass of pinot noir if you have it."

Cyril chuckled. "Of course we have it, dear Rasia. I am a winemaker, remember?"

Now Rasia blushed. "Of course. I guess it slipped

my mind."

Cyril composed himself a bit. "Relax. This promises to be a wonderful meal."

The servant reappeared with two glasses of pinot after a very short time, during which silence hung over the dining area. It was when things were so still that Rasia felt the most uncomfortable. It always gave her a feeling of powerlessness.

She took her wine glass and waved it gently beneath her nose, inhaling its scent deeply. Oh, it was rich and full-bodied! A smile crept across her face, and she closed her eyes to take a sip.

Cyril watched her closely. He gazed at her as she held the liquid in her mouth, swishing it over her tongue and languishing in its flavor. It was the most erotic thing he had ever watched a woman do, and he felt the tingle of an impending erection between his legs.

"You know wine," he stated in a husky tone.

Rasia opened her eyes and looked over the top of her wine glass at him. "I know a bit. You could call it a hobby."

DeSai smiled and straightened up in his chair, arranging his napkin over his lap as he did. "Let's begin, Rasia before it gets cold. Shall we?"

Soon they were eating, and DeSai gallantly initiated the conversation by bringing up his suggestions for their afternoon activities. "I thought we would stroll around some of the monuments, and I could tell you some of the nation's history. It will be nice to get to know you. Is there anything, in particular, you have an interest in seeing?"

"No," Rasia said. "I'll leave that up to you."

DeSai was reading her, but if she knew it, she did not let him know. Yes, she was holding herself back, but her eyes disagreed with her words. The distant attitude she exhibited did not matter to him, though it did keep him awake half the night. He had already decided that he would give her the special bite; she was the one he had chosen to be his queen, and soon she would know it. He had even considered simply biting her before making love to her, thereby sealing the deal, but he didn't want to ruin things. He wanted everything to be perfect so he would wait.

"Then that settles it," Cyril continued. "A 'monumental' stroll it will be."

The servant appeared with their plates, one at a time. The plates held beautifully glazed pork, garlic mashed potatoes, and roasted peppers, all of which melted in Rasia's mouth. After she had enjoyed a single bite of each dish on her plate, she began to relax; it was inevitable. She was enjoying some of the best food she had ever eaten, and she could feel the man at the table across from her adoring her with each second. Oh, to be indulged and worshipped for the rest of her life!

"President DeSai, did you always make wine?"

Cyril looked up from his dish with surprise. After a bit of thought, he nodded. "Yes, I always have made wine, just as the family that came before me."

Rasia took another bite of potato and took her time savoring it. "Have you always wanted to, I mean?"

Now DeSai put his fork down and wiped his mouth with his napkin. "I cannot remember a time when I didn't want to."

Her gaze did not falter. She continued to hold his eyes; she found herself interested in what he had to say, but she also had some much deeper questions.

"Then why run for the presidency?"

The two continued to stare at each other for a moment, and Cyril began to smile. "How about if I tell you all about it another time. There are very good reasons, but we should keep the spirit of the daylight, yes?"

Rasia nodded and returned his grin. They ate in silence, and soon the servant was once again at the table, this time to clear the plates. With hands full, he said, "For dessert, we have chocolate soufflé with vanilla ice cream. Will you enjoy hot coffee with your dessert?"

They both agreed, and soon they were quietly eating the homemade soufflé and ice cream. It went down very nicely as a topper to their meal, and the rich coffee hit the spot as well. Soon the entire meal was over, and Cyril turned to Rasia with an eager look as he stood.

"Are you ready to leave, my dear?"

Rasia stood as well, taking her purse off the table. "Yes, I am," she said. They had chatted a bit during the meal about a number of topics, and she had even told him about her father's death. She was feeling comfortable and loose with him now, and she hated herself for it, but the funny thing was she had no desire to put her guard up.

They walked around the Lincoln Memorial and the Reflecting Pool. They sat and talked at the Washington Monument, and he shared his childhood with her. He even told her about Cecile, but he spoke of her in modern terms. Before he knew it, he had told her about his entire life, or, at least, the parts which made things seem consistent with the times.

From there they visited the museum, which she found incredible and interesting. She decided that it was her favorite site of the day. By the time they wrapped up their tour, it was seven in the evening, and she was walking on air. He had managed to show her a wonderful time, and she was glad that Oleks had played hooky. Now they were in the limousine, and they were headed to her hotel.

He walked her to her room, and when they arrived at her door she stopped; she would not ask him in. He may have impressed her with his knowledge and company, but she would not give him an opportunity to ruin it all. Men always wanted to ruin everything.

But to her surprise, he didn't ask or insinuate that he wanted to join her. He took her hand and kissed it. "Thank you for your company today. I had the time of my life, and I mean that, Rasia."

She took back her hand and smiled slightly. "I had a good time as well, Mr. President."

"Please, I'm sure we can eliminate the formalities. Call me Cyril," he said. Would you like to attend the opera with me tomorrow evening, Rasia?"

She looked a bit confused for a moment, then said, "I will be checking out the morning after. It is probably not a good idea."

"Then come with me to Cliffside Wineries. I would love for you to see it and sample its wares. You will be seeing a real part of me in its workings, not to mention it is one of my favorite things to do." He smiled at her, his eyes filled with eager hope.

Rasia laughed. "Okay, Cliffside then. What time should I be ready?"

"I will send the car to fetch you at eight in the morning. We can have breakfast, I'll show you around the White House, and then we go out to the winery." He was thrilled that she was going to see him again. Tomorrow would be the day, he would see to it. He intended to turn on his full 'charm,' he would put her under his spell, now that she was so open to him.

He bowed slightly, his eyes glazed over a bit. "Sleep well tonight, my Rasia," he said, and once she was in her room with the door closed, he turned and walked away.

She tossed her purse onto the dresser and flopped down on her bed. For the next while, she stared at the ceiling and thought about President DeSai. He was definitely suave. He knew what to say and when to say it. He was persistent also, and this was a trait she admired. He was also gorgeous, but she could overlook that fact if it began to distract her too much.

The potential in the friendship they were forming knew no bounds. She fully intended to take advantage of every last bit of it for her own ends. She snickered a bit; if only he knew her real intentions. It then occurred to her that she wasn't even sure of her own intentions with him. Rasia was beginning to feel differently about DeSai than before.

While she was strongly attracted to him, Rasia felt no love; it was something she was incapable of. She would not allow the fact that she was a virgin have any influence on the situation. Sure, she was interested in what it would be like to have sex with someone like Cyril DeSai, but she didn't know what it was like to have sex with anybody, so what did it matter? Being a virgin would simply make it easier than ever for her to stand her ground and say no.

It would help her maintain her distance.

She rose off the bed and changed into pajama pants and a t-shirt. She then sat at the desk and began to review her outline, and she wrote details of her day with DeSai in her journal and notebook; there was much which could be added to her story. She tweaked the outline a bit and then tried to call her cameraman one last time before she shut off the lamp on the desk and got into bed.

Tomorrow would be a busy day.

∞

Cyril DeSai lay in his bed at the White House, his eyes wide open staring at the ceiling. Sleep would not come to him this night, of that he was certain. Rasia had been stunning today, and she was warming up to him quite nicely. He couldn't wait to see her again, and he certainly couldn't wait to have his hands all over that perfect little body of hers.

He began to think about her curves, the smell of her hair, and the sound of her voice, even when she was stern. He could not get her off his mind. Not only was she beautiful, but she also had the intelligence and attitude a queen of his would need. She was a bit harsh, and to him, that was a wonderful thing, the icing on the cake.

He would make her his, tomorrow, whether she liked it or not. If he could avoid controlling her mind to get the job done he would; he wanted her to be his willingly, but if he had to entice her, he would do that as well. He had no qualms about that whatsoever.

It was torture, but he would not ruin this with his own impatience. He needed to take her before it was time for her to return to Kiev, and so he would. He had inhaled her scent deeply all day, and she was as healthy as could be; he sensed no physical defects in her at all. Yes, tomorrow would be perfect for them both, from start to finish.

Finally, DeSai began to doze off, and he allowed sleep to have its way. The sooner he dreamed, the faster the morning would come, and then he could be with Rasia Engres again. Soon, he indeed was dreaming.

∞

DeSai and Engres were walking in an unknown park; he could even hear the buzzing of bees and see the colors of the flowers. He was holding her hand, and she was talking to him, telling him why she had decided to become a journalist. They came to a clearing, and he spread a blanket out on the ground; they sat down upon it.

He watched her as she spoke to him. She was telling him that she was able to control people without their knowledge by simply using her words. He was entranced; he certainly believed her, because she had control of him; that was for sure.

Then she said to him, "Let me show you what I mean: I love you, Cyril."

He felt his smile grow, and warmth spread all over his body. He leaned forward, and their lips met. Even in his dream, he could taste the sweetness of her lips! Oh, he had never, ever felt this way before!

Suddenly she pulled back from him. "It is my show to run; you are unnecessary," she said. He was confused. He didn't know what she was talking about at all.

Suddenly she opened her mouth, and it was full of pointed teeth, and he could see the blood of men dripping from each one. With an inhuman roar, she attacked him, and began to eat him alive…

DeSai woke with a shout and sat up in his bed. His normally cold body was sweating, and his heart was pounding in his chest. He had a nightmare, a horrible nightmare. He had not dreamed in years.

Love did funny things, he said to himself, and he smiled and pushed the dream out of his mind. In no time, he was sleeping like a baby.

R.W.K. Clark

CHAPTER 23

Rasia woke while it was still dark, thinking about Oleks. Where the heck had that kid gone? She got up and put her bathrobe on and grabbed both her key card and the one to his room, then she went out the door and over to his.

She opened his door and went in. Nothing appeared to have been used or touched at all except for his suitcase. She went into the bathroom and noticed he had showered before he had left, but otherwise, the room was spotless.

She left and went back to her own room, where she ordered coffee and some fruit through room service.

Rasia then dressed and sat at her desk. She got her laptop out and began to write her piece on Cyril DeSai, Oleks completely out of her mind now. She figured if he were going to be a butt, she would let him, but he certainly didn't have a job working with her anymore.

∞

DeSai woke the next morning and called Cliffside Wineries and spoke to Shirley Louis. "Good morning, love, how are things going for you now that I'm gone?"

His former assistant overflowed with excitement

when she heard the sound of his voice. She missed him, and he found it entertaining.

"Master! Things are good here, but we all wish we could see you more often. This new position of yours is going to be the death of us, I fear," she replied. He could hear that she was smiling by the sound of her voice, and he was entertained by her childlike eagerness.

He continued. "I'm sorry to hear that, but it is for the good of us all that this change has taken place. I plan to visit the winery with a friend today, and I wanted you to go into my office and make sure it is tidied up properly. I will have a guest with me" he said.

Cyril wanted today to be the final stage in his quest for Rasia. Nothing less than perfection at the winery would do, for he wanted her to see his soul, and the winery was his soul. Shirley knew all that he required, and he had full confidence that everything would be perfect when they arrived.

Shirley tried to dig a bit. "Who will you be bringing? New family?" Usually, the woman did not nose into his business at all, and the questions would have typically annoyed him, but he was in such good spirits that he didn't mind answering her at all.

"Shirley. I am bringing your future queen," he told her.

The statement was met with silence, and he knew that she was turning the information over in her head. None of his new family had any idea that he had spent his entire existence seeking one true mate, and he knew that learning this provided a whole new perspective about the existence of the species for them.

It was time they learned. They would need to honor Rasia as they honored him. He knew that jealousy would abound, but that was why Rasia's strong personality appealed to him so. Petty quarrels would not bother her in the slightest. She would shrug them off effortlessly, much like she had tried to do to him.

"It will all be fine, Shirley. You'll see, once she gets established, you will all have the mother-figure in your lives that you so desperately need," he said. "I'll let you get on with your day now, and I'll be seeing you this afternoon."

He hung up the phone just as Martin Lamb knocked at the door.

"President, the car is preparing to leave to fetch Ms. Engres. Will you be riding to get her?"

He shook his head and stood, straightening his tie as he did so. "No, Martin. I'll stay here and duck into the kitchen; I want to be sure they are preparing the quiche I requested properly."

The two men left the Oval Office and went their separate ways. DeSai realized he was humming to himself, and it amused him. When was the last time he had felt so… alive? He knew; it had been the day his wife died, so many years ago.

Finally, he had found what he had been looking for, and Master Cyril DeSai was more than ready to get on with the next chapter of his eternity.

Rasia had continued working on her article until seven, and then she stopped to get ready to go with DeSai for the day. She did her makeup first, then curled her hair into a casual look, moving some strands forward to compliment the shape of her face. She chose a simple white jersey dress and white pumps. She looked at her reflection in the full-length mirror in the bathroom and smiled. She outdid herself; she looked amazing.

She fully intended to use Cyril DeSai until there was nothing more to use. She was going to make out like a bandit on this deal; for all she knew, she wouldn't even need to worry about her career anymore. Becoming the editor of the 'Post' seemed like silliness to her now. She could feel it in her bones; she knew her future held incredible things for her now that she had met Cyril DeSai, and none of it had to do with love.

But she did feel something for the man, and it seemed to be growing. Well, what if she was growing fond of him? Wouldn't that only make the execution of all her plans more livable and enjoyable for her? She was sure, but it was certainly a very pleasing feeling.

She transferred the contents of her purse into a smaller white bag with gold metal embellishments, and then put on a pearl necklace and earrings. She grabbed up her key card and left her room, a smug smile of satisfaction on her face.

The ride to the White House was quiet and comfortable, and when they arrived, no Secret Service were waiting to escort her to the President. The driver simply asked her if she remembered how to get to the dining area and then took her to the elevator.

She walked into the dining room, and DeSai's eyes lit up immediately. "Hello! It is so good to see you. I was getting a bit anxious waiting. How has your morning been so far?"

"Very good," she replied. She couldn't help but smile at him; he was so pleased to see her. She approached him as he pulled her chair out, and she stopped before him. Rasia then leaned forward and kissed his cheek. "Thank you."

He felt his face flush at the touch of her lips, and for a fraction of a second, he thought his knees might buckle. This was going even better than he had hoped. He had no more expected her simple kiss than he expected her to take flight. He laughed to himself; soon enough she would be taking flight.

DeSai took his place and looked at her. "I hope you like quiche. You haven't eaten, have you?"

"I had a bit of fruit very early this morning, but I am ravenous now. Quiche sounds delicious," she replied. "I thought about you quite a bit last night, Mr. DeSai."

That got his attention. "What did you think about?"

Rasia played coy, smiling shyly as she unfolded her napkin. "I guess I enjoyed your company."

Cyril was beaming at this revelation, and even as the servant came into the room to serve the quiche, he stared at her and smiled.

Soon they were eating, and Rasia was being smooth

and entertaining. She gave him her full attention when he spoke, and she used humor like a weapon. She had him laughing freely, and she was laughing with him. She stopped avoiding his gaze, and she found that the more he looked at her, the freer she felt. DeSai was going to be a good time indeed.

After their meal, he took her on a full tour of the White House, showing her everything from the inner kitchen to the offices. Finally, he took her to his living quarters, and she was impressed with his taste. They relaxed on the terrace with mimosas, and they enjoyed each other's company immensely.

"How is your cameraman?" DeSai needed to play off the fact that the man had not been seen by him since they left their first night here. "Is he ill?"

Rasia smiled and took a sip of her drink. "He disappeared on me. I'm beginning to think he met a woman and decided he liked her company more than mine. I have to admit, I can be a bit of a dragon lady with those who work for me and with me."

"I'm sure you can." He chuckled at the fact. "Do you expect him to show back up at the last minute?" asked Cyril.

She shook her head. "To be honest, I couldn't care less if he did. He doesn't work for me anymore; I'm pretty sure he knows that."

"Yes, I'm sure he does," replied DeSai. "Well, on a lighter note, I called my previous assistant at the winery, and they are expecting us. Not only will you love Cliffside for the wine, Rasia, I believe the entire place will be a wonderful treat for you in all aspects."

She smiled. "Well, I must say I am relieved you asked me to your winery instead of offering to take me to the zoo."

This made Cyril laugh out loud, a rich, hearty laugh. "Your mind appeals to me so much, Rasia," he said. "I thought that today I would take you to Cliffside Wineries and show you its inner workings because I believe you will genuinely appreciate its workings. I am also very, very proud of my personal office there. It has some exquisite antiques. I have worked for many, many years to get the right aesthetic there."

"I am very much looking forward to the trip to your beloved winery, Cyril," she said. He took immediate notice of the fact that she called him by his first name, and it warmed his cold heart. He found himself hoping that he would hear her saying it for all eternity.

They each had another mimosa before taking a walk through the White House gardens. DeSai introduced her to every member of his staff that they encountered, and he made sure to include her in every conversation, no matter how small. She was swept off her feet by him, but it was not romantic in nature, of that Rasia was sure. She was impressed with his power, the way he carried himself, and the way those in his charge responded to his authority. Yes, this could be very good indeed.

"Rasia, I need to meet with my personal assistant briefly before we leave. Do you mind?" He had led her into his living space. "Feel free to watch television or listen to music if you like. I can also take you to the library if you'd rather wait there?"

Her eyes lit up; she did love books. "Yes, that would be wonderful," she replied, and with that, he led her off down the hall and into the library.

Rasia found the library to be quite beautiful and astounding. While Cyril was gone, she browsed the book collection there and found that there were some priceless items on the shelves. She touched their bindings, stroking some of her favorites as though they were old lovers. This had to be the best room she had been in so far at this place, and its existence made her never want to leave.

DeSai returned after about a half-hour. "Are you ready for our little journey?" he asked, and she simply nodded and took his arm.

"Do you like books, Cyril?" She was staring up at him, eagerly awaiting his response.

"Yes, but I don't get to read as much as I would like," he replied. "You are free to visit anytime you like, Rasia. Anytime at all."

As they walked to the chopper, DeSai came to the firm conclusion that he had made a wonderful choice in Rasia Engres.

CHAPTER 24

The helicopter ride to Cliffside was filled with conversation and laughter. If Cyril was not entertaining her with funny anecdotes, then Rasia was using her quirky brand of humor to impress him. So much did they laugh that they decided to stop during the trip and get some fresh air. Cyril made it a point to purchase a bouquet of flowers for Rasia, and he chose perfect orchids. He also bought a nosegay of daisies for Shirley Louis; it wouldn't do to not acknowledge her with her favorite flower.

Finally, the pair arrived at Cliffside. "The first thing on the agenda is to take you on the grand tour," Cyril announced. He took her by the hand as they walked up the main stairs to the entrance. "You will get to meet my dependable team, and you will get to taste and see why Cliffside makes what I consider to be the very best wine in the world."

Rasia found that she was beside herself with excitement. Could she have tracked down a more perfect male specimen? Rich, handsome, intelligent, and a lover of fine wine to boot? She was on cloud nine, even as he showed her the main building and introduced her to the staff as they encountered them.

It all could have been a dream, and it occurred to Rasia that she very well may be in love.

When they had been in every room in the main building, they went into the cellars where the wine was bottled and stored for aging. Here Rasia was able to sample as much wine as she wanted, and her first choice was the rich red Malbec.

"It is so delicious," she said as the warmth of the drink coursed through her body, and Cyril beamed with pride.

After giving her a nod, he said, "My reds are some of the finest on Earth. Do you prefer red over white, Rasia?"

"Absolutely," she replied. "The color alone is enough to mesmerize me. I will partake of white for the sake of the food being served, obviously, but when I imbibe socially, I choose reds."

This pleased him to no end. She would love what she would become then, of that much he was certain. The color of blood was very similar, and it tended to sparkle when it was in a glass as well. Once she was turned, it would be the aroma and flavor that she would love; she was that kind of woman.

After walking the grounds and seeing the vineyards, the two finally made their way back to the main building. With the tour over, Rasia would be getting hungry for dinner. Feeding her and letting her enjoy the wine would ensure that she felt completely comfortable with going to his office alone with him, and he was starting to believe that she was nearly there already. How her attitude had changed in the last few days! It was almost unbelievable.

He wanted to take her to his private office for more than sex. He wanted to tell her the truth. Cyril needed to test her responses to the hard reality of not only who and what he really was, but also what he expected her to become for him. He would indeed make love to her there, and he would administer the bite that would turn her.

Cyril held the door for Rasia as they entered the winery's main building, and for the second time that day, she was afforded a moment to admire the darkness and beauty of the art and sculpture which adorned the walls and pedestals in the entryway. She had always had a taste for the macabre and seeing how Cyril did as well pleased her very much. His taste was fully exquisite, and it came out of him in every way possible.

Once they reached the dining area, they were flooded with the royal treatment once again, even more than they were at the White House. It seemed every time she turned around, someone was at her elbow filling her wine glass, clearing her plate, or asking if she needed anything. She was overwhelmed by the attention and the plush surroundings. She found herself wondering for a fleeting moment what it would be like if all of this was hers and hers alone. Well, it was far too early to get ahead of herself she knew.

Cyril, on the other hand, was completely enraptured with the woman before him. While he was at a loss as to how she affected him the way she did, he was too happy to care about his confusion. He wanted to impress her; he wanted to possess her. Every word he said, anything he did, was motivated in pleasing Rasia Engres. He drifted off in thought more than once, considering what her sweet love would be like.

They dined on rare Porterhouse steaks, baked potatoes, and fresh sweet corn off the cob. When the server had asked Rasia how she wanted her steak, she had ordered hers rare before Cyril had ordered his own the same, and his heart skipped a beat.

"A woman after my own heart," said Cyril, watching her closely. "I have never met one who liked her meat the same way I do. What about it do you enjoy, may I ask?"

Rasia smiled and looked him in the eye. "I like to taste the death, Cyril."

His lips curled into a somewhat evil smile. This woman was far more than perfect; she was made for him and him alone.

They ate in silence, but DeSai couldn't stop sneaking looks at her during the meal. She seemed oblivious to his own presence, however, but this didn't bother the Master at all. Soon enough he would be her sole obsession.

But Rasia knew that he was there; she could practically feel the force of his existence! She wanted to share herself with him, the Rasia that no one was aware existed. The evil, self-indulgent, and cruel woman that she really was. How would he respond to her? Surely he would wash his hands of Rasia Engres right away.

At the very end of the meal, she was introduced to Shirley Louis, the administrative assistant. The woman was cordial, and even tried to be warm, but Rasia was very familiar with the 'catty' behavior of other females, especially around her. She sensed it in Shirley, and it pleased her.

As they walked back down the hall to the main entrance, Cyril took her down another corridor to the right. "I almost forgot to show you the winery museum and gift shop. It is filled with family artifacts, as well as mementos for the tourists to buy," he said, his voice eager. "We recently located both to this wing, and I often forget about them."

The museum was filled with historical items, though family documents and memorabilia seemed a bit vague and scant to Rasia. As he showed her grainy photos and paperwork, she took note that his ancestors were nearly all named Cyril, and she brought it up.

"Yes," he explained. "It is our tradition to name the firstborn son after the father." He would not tell her the whole truth until they were safely in the office below. The truth that revealed the fact that all of them were, in reality, he himself.

The gift shop was what one would expect. It was simple and sold souvenirs for the public. The winery was usually open to the public for tours seven days a week, but he made her aware that he had called off touring for the day so she could visit and they could have the place to themselves.

They went into a plush conference room next, located near the front of the building. Here he pulled out a seat for her and then proceeded to pour them both another glass of wine.

"Shiraz, this time Rasia," Cyril said as he held a full glass out to her. "I believe it is your preference?"

"Cyril, if I didn't know better I would think you were trying to get me drunk," she said to him, a sexy smile on her face.

"My dear, you are a smart one indeed." He would not start his eternity with this woman with lies; he simply used his own humor and agreed. "I have horses here. Let's take a carriage ride, shall we?"

They both drank the Shiraz, quickly draining their glasses, then Cyril filled her glass with a nice merlot, and they made their way through the building, coming out in a large pasture. It was fenced, and there was a large stable building to one side. Cyril took Rasia by the hand and smiled. "This should be very romantic. Have you ever taken a carriage ride through the countryside before?"

"No, I haven't," she said. She took another sip of her wine and began to walk with him toward the stables.

The carriage was ready for them when they arrived; he was an exceptional planner. In minutes, she was seated on quilted satin on a carriage that looked to be hundreds of years old, yet it could have just been made, it was in such perfect condition.

"You are a collector of many things, are you not?" she asked him, looking at him closely.

He stared back at her smiling. Then they took off out of the stables like a shot, the wind in their faces.

Cyril DeSai was head over heels in love, and Rasia Engres was right on his heels.

R.W.K. Clark

CHAPTER 25

They rode the carriage all along the countryside around the winery. He showed her a variety of things, from some of the cliffs to the sands of the seashore. He showed her trees and birds, and they sat in the grass together talking and laughing for most of the early afternoon.

It was then, seated on the grass under a massive willow, that Rasia Engres came to a very strong realization: she was, most definitely, in love with Cyril DeSai, winemaker and president of the United States of America. She knew with certainty that this was exactly what the emotion felt like, and it was intoxicating.

Now it was time to return to the winery, and Rasia was getting excited to see his office. While she didn't have a particular knowledge of antiques, she knew that his taste in art was outstanding. If his office décor was anything like the things he had displayed in the corridors, she was in for a treat indeed.

During the carriage ride back, she began to speak to him about her days as a girl, but she kept things superficial. She didn't bring up her parents because she didn't want her voice to give away the hatred she felt for them. Instead, she told him about how she came to study journalism, and she even indulged a bit of her future aspirations to him. She was trusting him, and she felt a rush at the intimacy. What had she been missing her whole life?

Now they walked up a long hallway, the elevator waiting for them at the end. "How do you like it, Rasia?" asked DeSai.

"It's the most wonderful place I have ever seen," she replied.

They got on the elevator, and as soon as the doors closed, she wrapped her arms around his neck and looked him in the eye. "I know I haven't been the most pleasant during our time together, and I apologize for that. My history has established many of my moods, you see. I am apprehensive with all that I meet."

He lowered his head quickly and covered her mouth with his; she let him do this, and reveled in his taste, as he did hers. They explored each other's mouths with great hunger, and for the first time in her life, Rasia felt the powerful tingle between her legs. This was no longer only about her own agenda. She knew she wanted to be with him, enjoying his company and ruling the most powerful country in the world.

But Cyril was thinking about other things. He tasted something in her he had never tasted in a woman before: evil, pure and simple. She had a heart as black as his. The only thing separating them was that he would live forever, and until he had her and bit her as he planned, she would not. Otherwise, he learned one thing of major importance from that kiss: she had no defect in her except for her black, black soul.

To Cyril DeSai, that made her perfect.

The next place they ventured into was floors below. They had spent ten full minutes kissing in the elevator before he was able to push the button, and now she stood wondering where they were going. Cyril knew that this was the ultimate test, her visiting his office. It was on the lowest floor of the winery, a full four stories underground. It was very morbid in décor, and it was dark and foreboding to most. If she could handle it down there, she could handle him.

"Are you going to show me your office?" she asked him, eager like a child.

He smiled. "Yes," he replied. "I thought we could have some wine and talk for a while, Rasia. How does that sound to you?"

"Perfect," she purred. "I have so looked forward to seeing it since you told me about it."

The elevator came to a stop, and the doors slowly opened.

Rasia sucked air into her lungs sharply, and DeSai looked over at her to read her face. He was pleased to see her eyes were alight and her smile was broad.

"Yes," she said. "It is amazing. Even better than I could have possibly imagined."

She stepped out of the elevator as if in a daze; she had never seen a place so beautiful in all her life. They were only in a hallway, but that hallway was Rasia herself, her very depths and soul. It was astounding.

The walls were done in black and red. The background, which was black, was covered with red skulls. From a distance, they looked to be spattered with blood, and it was only with attention one could see the gorgeous details within. They were almost three-dimensional, and they took her breath away as they seemed to move and dance.

There were sconces with black candles spaced in even increments all down the walls. The candles were lit, and they flickered brilliantly, adding to the effect. The flames themselves appeared to be blood-red.

There were also sculptures on pedestals down the length of the corridor. These were nothing one could view at a typical museum; they were of murder and death. One depicted a demon eating the heart directly from the chest of a lifeless damsel; another showed a gargoyle-like creature on his hands and knees, his head thrown back as he screamed in the direction of the sky. He was as angry as Rasia herself had been her entire life.

"Oh, Cyril," was all she could say. "You have read my heart."

Yes, he thought to himself. She was perfect. The black heart within her beckoned loudly to his own.

Now she took notice of the black double doors at the very end of the hall. She turned to him and asked, "Is that it?"

"Yes."

She turned to him fully. "Cyril, I need to tell you something."

She had left that morning with the full intent of

never sleeping with this man. Even now, she felt nothing more than intrigue for the man standing before her, but she felt something else pulling at her, and it was powerful. She felt it at her breasts and between her legs.

It was lust.

"Rasia, my darling, there is nothing you cannot tell me," Cyril replied.

She lowered her eyes. "I am a virgin," she told him.

Now he was overcome. He thought he had been given everything, but he discovered that he had been wrong. He wouldn't have dared ask for a mate who had never been touched by another, not in this day and age. But here she was. She would be his entirely. His hunger piqued.

"We will not rush, my beautiful Rasia. Don't be nervous or afraid; we will talk, we will become more familiar with each other."

She looked up at him. "I am not afraid, Cyril. I simply have no… experience."

"That is not for you to worry about, my Rasia," he said in a husky voice. "You leave that all up to me."

He took her by the hand, and they began toward the double-doors of the office. When they reached it, he let go of her hand long enough to put his key in the lock and open the doors; he thrust them both inward at the same time.

What she saw with her eyes won her soul.

The walls of his office's interior were even more dark and sinister than those in the hall. They told an entire story, from beginning to end, of someone whose life was stolen from him in a single night. She could see the story with her eyes. It too was red on black, and she suddenly realized that all the red she saw was blood.

The walls were decorated in blood. As sure as she was standing in Cyril DeSai's private office at Cliffside, she knew that what she saw was blood.

He had antique mahogany furniture, hand carved, all over the office. A black long-haired cat sat perched on an ancient ottoman of mahogany and black leather. The light of the fireplace danced off its green eyes.

She walked around the room, which was lit only by candles, and touched everything, stroking paintings and sculptures as though they were lovers. Rasia stared at the contents of the office, taking her time with each and every one, soaking up as much of the beautiful information as each piece would give her. Finally, after a long time, she turned to DeSai and spoke.

"Who are you, Cyril DeSai?" she asked him, a look of wide-eyed wonder on her face. "What are you?"

He had no idea she already knew.

He stepped fully into the room and closed the doors behind him, locking them securely. "Let's have a glass of wine, my Rasia, and we will talk about that. Does that sound okay to you?"

She sat on one of two chaise lounges which were situated before the fireplace and allowed herself to recline. She kicked her shoes to the floor and stretched out her long legs. She knew she had arrived; this is where she belonged.

So why did she feel so much emotion for this

perfect man?

He poured two glasses of the aged Shiraz she had loved so much and walked to her. He handed her one glass, then took his place on the other chaise lounge. He would not overwhelm her, at least not right away. He would wait until she knew his truth.

"I want to tell you the story of my life, but before I do, I want to tell you that I do not expect you to accept what you are going to hear. The truth is no one could. It is my hope you will be the first, and willingly share my life with me," DeSai began.

Rasia held his gaze steadily. She knew, as she knew her own name that what he was going to tell her was going to change life as she knew it forever, and she was completely prepared. She had her suspicions. All the revelation would do was solidify her resolve.

"I want you to be willing to share it with me," Cyril continued. "That is what will make you different from all the rest in the end. Do you understand?"

She nodded. "I am ready to hear anything you have to say, Cyril. I am listening."

The Master nodded and began.

First, he told her about his childhood in France, and his father, a winemaker. He told her every detail, leaving out only the year of his birth. Next, he related to her the story of meeting his beloved Cecile. He shared how they danced and made love in the moonlight, and how he never expected to find another who made him feel the way Cecile had.

Now he moved on to his children. This was difficult

for him to share, simply for the fact that he had buried their memory so deeply in his mind that recalling it was like slicing himself wide open. He shed no tears as he talked, however; his body no longer made them.

Finally, he began to tell her about the fateful night when he had been turned. He told her about the damaged row of grapes and the pile of dead dogs. He told her about Marquis, Cecile, and the bloody mess that had been made of his children.

Rasia listened intently and did not interrupt him once, but her mind was moving a thousand miles an hour. She knew. She figured out within the first five minutes of him talking who and what he was. She nailed it when he slipped up and mentioned riding into the vineyards with his father on a wagon.

This man was a vampire. Yes, it would have been the only explanation.

This was why they all loved and catered to him; he was literally in control of the entire country, no, the world. This was how he won the Presidential election by a landslide; this was why he was so… perfect.

By the time he had finished telling her his story, she knew she was right, and he confirmed it with his own words. "I will never die, Rasia. I am destined to walk this forsaken planet forever, without love, without sadness, without ever feeling true joy. I am eternal, and I am alone."

"You are a vampire, Cyril," Rasia said quietly.

"Yes…"

She sat up on the lounge. "All of the photos in the

museum, they were all you…?"

"Yes."

Rasia then lowered her voice. "You will live forever?"

"Eternity."

She stood and crossed over to him, sitting beside him on the lounge. She touched his face gently with her fingers, stroking his cheek. He was a handsome man, and she knew that she was in love with him, at least as much as a woman like her could be. No, she would not settle for less; she would have what he had.

"Now it's my turn," she said. "I will tell you the truth about myself."

And, as Cyril had, she told him her own story. She told him of killing the man at eleven, and how it had filled her with ecstasy. She told him of every evil she had ever done, and there were many. She also related to him the truth about her career and the secret desires of her heart regarding power and success. She told him of her mother, who she was pleased to hear had died when she did.

She did omit some of the more important details, details which explained her ancestry. Details that justified her hardness and distance from others. Very important details.

Details which may have made Cyril reconsider his choice to make Rasia Engres his queen.

Now she looked at Cyril DeSai and spoke with an honesty that was terribly brutal. "I don't know if I love you, but I want to be yours. I must say that my motive is less than pure. I don't want to be mastered, I want to master. If you want to share your life with me, I will willingly give you mine."

What she said no longer mattered to his choice. He would take her regardless, but having her willingness was nothing short of miraculous to him. He wanted it all to be perfect, and thus far it was. He could only imagine what their future together would hold for the both of them, for the family, and for the world.

Cyril listened to her words closely. His heart sank a bit when she told him she thought she lacked love for him, but he knew that in the end that didn't matter at all. What he wanted she longed to give him. He would give her what she wished for: eternal life, riches, and power.

"Do you understand you will spend eternity completely empty? You will be only a shell?" Cyril asked her.

She smiled at him. "Do you understand that I am empty already? You would only be filling me up."

With cat-like speed and grace, he grabbed her by the back of her head and pulled her mouth to his. He then began to run his hands over her entire body, and he was just a bit rough as he did, testing the waters with this woman. She pushed him away, smiling, and let the rest of her hair down. It fell all around her head in long jumbled curls. He was going to have so much fun with Rasia, his breathtaking virgin.

Now she stood and rid her body of the dress she wore. Beneath she had white panties and a white bra.

The sight of this female in pure white drove him nearly mad. She reached behind her and unhooked her bra and threw it into the fire; it burned up almost instantly.

Now she walked back to him and straddled him, sitting right on top of his groin. He was as hard as a rock. She reached down and began to unbutton his shirt. When she was done, she flung it open and looked at his chest. He was well muscled, and his chest was free of hair. That pleased her, as hairy men were disgusting in her sight.

Now she stood again and began to remove her panties. He rose like a flash and rid himself of all his clothing. They looked at each other in the firelight. She was perfect; her stomach was flat, her bottom well-rounded. Her breasts were the perfect size for her form, and they were topped with hard, pink nipples that he wanted to taste.

He was physical perfection from head to toe, and she realized her crotch was growing wet. Virgin or not, this man would have her this night. She knew she had won before they even began; the world was hers for the taking, literally.

When their eyes met, Rasia smiled, and suddenly she rushed toward him. She kissed him with passion, running her tongue over his teeth. She bit at his lips and ran her long nails down his back. He groaned loudly with great pleasure, and he melted in her arms.

After letting her go mad on him for a bit, he lifted her off the ground and threw her down on the lounge. He spread her legs forcefully, and she laughed at him, pleased with his roughness. He smiled before putting his head between her legs.

He held nothing back there, except he did not penetrate her with his fingers or tongue; he would save that.

He made her come over and over again; she had never experienced anything like it. She responded violently to his touch, thrusting herself against his face, clawing and scratching, demanding more and more… and more.

Finally, Cyril mounted her and put the head of his penis against her wetness. He did not intend to be gentle, and she did not want him to. They looked at each other in the firelight, and both of them smiled evil, lustful smiles.

With one quick thrust, he was inside of her. She cried out at first, but then her laughter began. She took hold of his rear and drove him deeper into her as she ground herself against him. The sound of their sweating skin slapping together filled the room, and he knew he could not hold back any longer.

He buried his face in her neck, and just as she reached yet another climax, he bit down. He let his venom enter her bloodstream, and then he pulled away, his own orgasm upon him, wracking his body.

They both began to shake, Cyril with great pleasure, Rasia with the turning. They lay trembling, DeSai on top of his new queen, feeling her womanhood clenching down on him. He held her tightly as her body convulsed as the venom took over.

It was happening very, very quickly. He had never given this bite, and now he knew it was something that took complete control in only minutes. He was thrilled.

When she stopped trembling, she was completely still. He raised himself and looked into her eyes. "Are you okay, my Rasia?" feeling the closest thing to love he had felt in centuries.

"Yes, Cyril. I couldn't be more perfect," she said with an eerie calmness. Rasia looked him in the eye.

Something in her voice was different, it was sinister. His heart began to pound, and he watched her closely.

She leaned forward, and putting her hands in his hair, she kissed him with great passion. Then, she wound his hair around her fingers tightly and ripped his head from his body. It happened in only seconds. His body fell lifeless to the rug between the lounges, blood leaking from his neck. She looked down at the head in her hands and reveled in the look of surprise that was forever plastered on the dead Master's face. His eyes were wide open, staring back.

R.W.K. Clark

EPILOGUE

Rasia DeSai sat at the desk in the Oval Office at the White House in Washington, DC. She was the first female president of the United States of America, having come into power by succeeding her dead husband, who had been the Master of the world.

Now they catered to her; there were no arguments, there was no confusion. As soon as she had turned, every vampire in the world knew it. They had a new queen, and the Master was gone. She was merciless and drove them all like slaves. She had a very bright future indeed. Her dreams had all come true.

So, in her selfishness, she had Cyril, she took advantage of his love for her. She seduced him, and she let him have her, and then she took not only his power, but she stole his very life. Then the black-hearted witch reveled in all he had earned, all of his power and possessions, acting as though she were entitled.

She realized she adored and missed him, Cyril DeSai, her kindred spirit. Oh, how they had been alike! Oh, how she had ruined her own future in only the passing of a second after their heated, and only, a moment of passion.

But he would not leave the Earth without leaving some of himself. No, that would be far too easy now, wouldn't it?

Even as I record these words in the pages of this precious Book, I can hear the anger and hatred in them. She worked so long and so hard for what she thought to be her destiny, only to discover that she, like Cyril, and like the puppets that were her 'family,' were being used. There was so much more to the story than she, or anyone before her, had ever known or understood.

I sit in the greatest house on the planet, the White House in the United States of America, as I write these sacred words. I think about how vital this portion of history is to record; it must be done with great care, and with great caution. For the first time in my life, tears fall from my eyes, for in retrospect I clearly see what a puppet I truly am, that Cyril was, that the entire population of the world has always been. I am sickened and terrified by this truth. But regardless of the truth, the end will remain the same.

My own existence and position were given to me solely for the purpose of that day, and the knowledge of that fact nearly kills me inside, but I must remain true to my personal heritage: I am a witch, and I must surrender to it in submission.

ENTREATY

This book was made possible by reviews from readers like you. Reviews fuel my creativity. If you enjoyed this novel, I implore you to please write a review and share your experience on the retailer's website. The livelihood for authors is entirely dependent on reviews, and I must say, it is the largest obstacle as a struggling author that I have encountered. Please tell a friend, tell a loved one about this read. With your help, I will be one step closer to overcoming this obstacle. In return, I thank you from the bottom of my heart, and sincerely appreciate your time and effort.

Humbled, with gratitude,

R.W.K. Clark

ABOUT THE AUTHOR

I am a father of two beautiful children, Jon and Kim. They are my motivating forces; they are the lighthouse in this vast ocean. In my life, they are the air that I breathe; they are the oasis in this desert of uncertainty. They are my greatest joy in life and my number one priority. I have a long list of hobbies, and I attribute that to my lust for life! I like to surround myself with positive people, who share the same interests. Family values, the arts, outdoors, nature, and travel are tops on my list. I embrace attending cultural and artistic events because I believe dramatic self-expression is the window to the soul. I wear my heart on my sleeve, and I still believe in chivalry, and I always treat people the way I want to be treated.

www.rwkclark.com